The bikers drew closer, their weapons leveled

"Down! Now!" the Executioner barked.

Instead Helena leaned forward, reaching for her purse. Bolan didn't shift his gaze from the rearview mirror and the open road before him, but from the corner of his eye he saw the woman reach into her bag and withdraw a palm-sized .22 automatic.

"What do you think you're doing?" the warrior demanded.

"Just what it looks like," she countered, releasing the gun's safety.

At that moment a round blew out the front tire. The Mustang lurched to one side, and Bolan fought the wheel, trying to correct the drift. But it was impossible to thwart the speeding vehicle's momentum, and the Executioner knew better than to risk flipping the car by slamming on the brakes.

As the Mustang began to go into a tailspin, the warrior shouted, "Stay loose and roll with it . . . we're going to crash!"

MACK BOLAN.

The Executioner

DON PENDLETON'S
THE EXECUTIONER®
FEATURING MACK BOLAN®

SHIFTING TARGET

A GOLD EAGLE BOOK FROM
WORLDWIDE®

TORONTO • NEW YORK • LONDON
AMSTERDAM • PARIS • SYDNEY • HAMBURG
STOCKHOLM • ATHENS • TOKYO • MILAN
MADRID • WARSAW • BUDAPEST • AUCKLAND

ISBN 0-373-61181-1

Special thanks and acknowledgment to
Ron Renauld for his contribution to this work.

SHIFTING TARGET

There is no calamity greater than lavish desires.
There is no greater guilt than discontentment.
And there is no greater disaster than greed.
                                    —Lao-tzu
                                    ca. 604–ca. 531 B.C.

A man enslaved by money and a burning desire to
acquire more at all costs will come to grief. You can
take that to the bank.
                                    —Mack Bolan

THE
MACK BOLAN®
LEGEND

Nothing less than a war could have fashioned the destiny of the man called Mack Bolan. Bolan earned the Executioner title in the jungle hell of Vietnam.

But this soldier also wore another name—Sergeant Mercy. He was so tagged because of the compassion he showed to wounded comrades-in-arms and Vietnamese civilians.

Mack Bolan's second tour of duty ended prematurely when he was given emergency leave to return home and bury his family, victims of the Mob. Then he declared a one-man war against the Mafia.

He confronted the Families head-on from coast to coast, and soon a hope of victory began to appear. But Bolan had broken society's every rule. That same society started gunning for this elusive warrior—to no avail.

So Bolan was offered amnesty to work within the system against terrorism. This time, as an employee of Uncle Sam, Bolan became Colonel John Phoenix. With a command center at Stony Man Farm in Virginia, he and his new allies—Able Team and Phoenix Force—waged relentless war on a new adversary: the KGB.

But when his one true love, April Rose, died at the hands of the Soviet terror machine, Bolan severed all ties with Establishment authority.

Now, after a lengthy lone-wolf struggle and much soul-searching, the Executioner has agreed to enter an "arm's-length" alliance with his government once more, reserving the right to pursue personal missions in his Everlasting War.

1

Mack Bolan shifted his weight, trying to relax muscles cramped from several hours of surveillance. The warrior was concealed amid an overgrowth of wild hedges in a field across from the main entrance to Gerley Chemical Corporation, a major defense contractor specializing in weapons research, particularly in the field of biochemical warfare. Someone inside the sprawling complex was stealing not only classified information about Gerley's biochemical and germ-warfare research, but also significant amounts of the various compounds used in testing. The thefts were alarming enough, but it had recently come to the attention of the U.S. intelligence community that both stolen documents and supplies had found their way onto the black market, where they had been snatched up by a Bolivian rebel force headed by Jax Allmus, a longtime rival of neighboring Colombia's infamous Medellín cartel. It was widely known that Allmus was out to wrest control of the South American cocaine market, which was reported up for grabs after the drubbing the Medellín cartel had received in recent years by various factions, including the U.S. military.

It was feared that, if given the chance, the Bolivians would inevitably use the materials either to snuff out what was left of the cartel or, more disturbingly, to barter them to anti-American terrorist factions in exchange for aid in establishing their own global distribution network for cocaine.

Undercover agents had been placed inside Gerley's three-acre facility in Talville, Michigan, for the past six weeks, but the only significant breakthrough was the accidental discovery, earlier that day, of some stolen research papers concealed in a plastic tube and hidden in the woods adjacent to the employee parking lot. The papers, surprisingly, dealt not with biochemical warfare studies, but with new developments in drugs related to the treatment of schizophrenia and other mental disorders. Similar papers, and some of the sample drugs used in experimental phases of the studies, had been reported missing in recent months, but the assumption had always been that the thefts, like those involving pharmaceutical cocaine, were likely attributable to personnel with drug-abuse problems and not part of some grander scheme. Now, however, there was concern that perhaps the same parties were involved in both threats, which posed the possibility that somewhere out there was a foe considering not only "conventional" biochemical terrorism, but also some diabolical plot to create a warfare agent that would attack a victim's mental capacities as well as his respiratory and circulatory systems. The only way to determine if such a scenario was being considered would be to not only sniff out the person or persons stealing the documents and supplies in question, but also to track down the party or parties receiving the contraband.

Theorizing that the woods might well be a drop site used by the traitor working for Gerley Chemical, a switch had been made, substituting the papers with falsified data and replacing the container where it had been found. Bolan's assignment was to monitor the drop site until there was a pickup, then to follow the courier in hopes of being led to the head of the espionage operation.

Bolan wasn't working alone. Pilots in four separate helicopters were staking out perimeters on the outskirts of Talville, ready to move in and assist in aerial surveillance once the chase was on. Closer at hand was Don White, a fifteen-year veteran of the Detroit police department's heralded antiterrorist strike force. Positioned sixty yards away in a tree, he had an unobstructed view of the drop site. To aid in his surveillance, White's Marlin 336 CS rifle was equipped with a high-powered infrared night scope. In the event that it became necessary to contend with the enemy there at the drop site, White was a renowned marksman.

Both Bolan and White had walkie-talkies to keep each other posted on any suspicious activity, but so far neither man had found reason to contact the other or the copter crews. It had been a waiting game, with a slow, grinding sense of anticipation.

It was now approaching midnight. The graveyard shift was already on duty, and most of those who'd been on the job from three to eleven had already left the parking lot. Bolan had hoped that there would be an attempted pickup during the shift change, but no one had strayed from the parking lot into the woods.

Bolan let his gaze drift from the drop site to the eastern horizon, some twenty miles away. He still couldn't believe what he was seeing.

The Detroit skyline was aglow with flame.

The warrior could count at least fifteen separate bonfires blazing into the night sky, two more than fifteen minutes ago. It looked like war had broken out, but Bolan knew it was only the revelry of Devil's Night, a grim Halloween tradition in Motown. Vandals roamed the streets with impunity, torching vacant buildings and howling in triumph whenever the fires took hold. More often than not the blazes had a way of getting out of hand, and there was rarely a year when charred corpses weren't found amid smoldering rubble in the wake of the "celebration." Police and civic leaders alike had lobbied fiercely in recent years to quell the ritual arson, and they'd succeeded to some extent... until this year.

From the looks of it, Bolan guessed the destruction was the worst in recent memory and might very well end up rivaling the carnage witnessed during the race riots of the 1960s. It seemed incredible that a citizenry would inflict such wanton devastation upon itself.

Suddenly the night was rent by an explosion, not more than a hundred yards away. Bolan whirled at the sound, staring into the woods behind him. There was a second blast, even more forceful than the first, and through the dense growth of trees he could see a burst of flames at the edge of a nearby trailer park. Then, as the booms were still echoing through the forest, the Executioner heard a woman scream, coming from the same direction as the fire.

Rising from his knees, the warrior emerged from the hedge and keyed his microphone.

"I'm going to check that out," he told White. "Keep an eye on things here."

"Gotcha," White responded over the receiver's palm-sized speaker. "Careful..."

As he rushed into the woods, Bolan reached inside his coat and withdrew the Beretta automatic from its armpit sling. Something told him the inferno on the other side of the forest had nothing to do with Halloween.

HELENA SIMMONS had been conducting her own surveillance that evening, stationing herself at the edge of the other side of the forest, within sight of the trailer park. Her focus had been on the trailer home situated closest to the trees, the same trailer that had, without warning, been rocked by the two explosions.

The woman was unarmed, and when she broke from her cover to approach the blazing trailer, she wasn't prepared to defend herself when a man wearing a ski mask suddenly rose in front of her, materializing as if he'd sprouted from the leaf-strewed ground.

Her startled scream was involuntary, and short-lived as well. The man clamped his hand over her mouth as he circled behind her and prodded the barrel of a .22-caliber pistol against her ribs.

"Shut up!" he seethed into her ear.

She could smell gasoline on the man's fingers. Her mind raced, trying to piece it all together. This guy must have set fire to the trailer, that much seemed certain. He had probably been knocked to the ground by the force of the explosion, and she'd surprised him by arriving so suddenly. He was most likely eager to leave the scene and not inclined to leave behind a witness with a chance, however remote, of identifying him.

"You're coming with me!" he commanded, jerking the woman off balance as he started down a dirt path leading into the dark forest. She struggled and stumbled a few times as he dragged her alongside him. The man was strong enough to hold her up without being pulled off stride, but she was clearly slowing him down.

Soon Helena could hear the rippling current of Long Noise River, a wide ribbon of water that ran through the heart of the forest. There were picnic grounds along the embankment, and although the park had been closed for hours, a light still glowed atop a pedestrian bridge spanning the river.

They were halfway across the bridge when the man suddenly stopped, wrenching Helena around with so much force she felt something snap in her shoulder and shoot daggers of pain up into her skull and down the length of her left arm. She let out a muffled cry, not only because of the injury but also because she found herself staring at a second gunman, this one just about to step onto the bridge. He was barely in range of the bridge's light, but Helena could see that he was tall, dark-haired and wore blue-on-black fatigues. Her first thought was that it was an accomplice, but she quickly realized that she'd been jerked around to serve as a human shield.

"Let her go and drop your gun!" the other man advised Helena's captor.

"Not a chance! How about *you* drop *your* gun, right now!"

"That's not going to—"

"Do it or she dies!"

BOLAN HAD BEEN in situations like this before, and he knew there was no set response. In some instances he'd felt his opponent was either bluffing or too slow at the trigger to carry out his threat, and in those cases he'd refused to give up his gun, instead opting to take his best shot. A hostage had never been wounded by Bolan, and in every case the gunman had been either killed on the spot or disabled enough to be apprehended without having a chance to fire his weapon.

In a few fleeting seconds, Bolan determined that this wasn't one of those situations. The man in the ski mask had positioned himself too securely behind the woman, offering little target area. Equally crucial, the hammer was back on his gun and the barrel was nuzzled against the woman's throat. Even if by some miracle Bolan was to get off a shot that would kill the man instantly, the gun was still apt to go off, and there were few wounds more fatal than a bullet through the jugular or carotid artery.

So the warrior took the only course he felt was viable. Slowly extending his arm from his side, he let go of his Beretta. The gun landed in the leaves at his feet.

Bolan might have left himself unarmed, but he wasn't unprepared. As the gunman suddenly leaned away from his prisoner and turned his gun on Bolan, the Executioner was already in motion, leaping sideways. The gunshot whizzed past him as he dived toward a nearby fallen oak. A second bullet chewed at the decaying bark near his head as he crawled behind the cover of the thick trunk.

The warrior stayed put, out of his would-be assassin's view. He lay still, trying to gauge the masked man's next move, and finally he heard footsteps on the bridge.

Another shot rang out, then the shattering of glass as the lone light on the bridge died out, plunging the woods into darkness. At the sound of struggling on the bridge, Bolan sprang to his feet and rushed toward his fallen gun. As he snatched it up, he heard the woman let out another scream, this one stifled when she toppled headlong into the river.

The Executioner's eyes hadn't adjusted enough to the darkness to be able to pick out the gunman on the bridge. When he heard retreating footsteps he raised his gun and rattled off a 3-round burst. All the shots missed, as did the gunfire returned by the assailant once he'd cleared the bridge and was on the other side of the river.

Although he would have liked to pursue, Bolan's first concern was for the woman. He'd heard no further screams after she'd hit the water, and there was no indication that she had surfaced or begun swimming out of the current's grasp.

Unclipping his walkie-talkie, Bolan quickly relayed word of what had happened to Don White, adding, "It's just a hunch, but this might be our guy."

"I'll be ready for him," White replied.

Bolan quickly scrambled down the steep embankment to the river's edge, where he kicked off his shoes and holstered his Beretta as he scanned the dark waters for a trace of the woman. Finally he spotted her, facedown in the middle of the river, being carried along like a piece of driftwood.

The warrior waded a few feet out until the water was up past his knees, then dived forward, taking care not to angle too deeply. The moment he came up for air, he began stroking his arms and legs in smooth, steady movements, inching toward the woman. The water was cold and he was weighed down by his wet clothes, but he concentrated solely on getting to the woman.

Some thirty yards downriver another fallen tree had created a snag of gathered litter and debris. When the woman was carried past, her arm tangled in one of the tree limbs. It was a tenuous obstruction, but it kept her in place long enough for Bolan to catch up.

Flipping the woman on her back, the warrior swam to the trunk and hoisted her partially out of the water. Once he had her head propped back, he checked to make sure she wasn't breathing, then began to perform artificial resuscitation.

After close to a minute the woman responded, coughing up water as she gasped for air. Frantic and disoriented, she began flailing her arms, nearly falling back into the water as she pushed away from Bolan.

"Hey, easy," he told her. "Easy..."

Once she opened her eyes and blinked out the water, she recognized Bolan and stopped fighting him. Between coughs, she sputtered, "What happened?"

"Let's get on dry land first, then we can sort things out," Bolan suggested. "Okay?"

Helena nodded. Bolan followed the tree toward the far riverbank, helping the woman along beside him. Once they reached shallow water, they let go of the tree and trudged ashore. Helena collapsed to the ground with another coughing jag. Bolan crouched beside her. Once she'd cleared her lungs and sat up, he asked her, "Are you all right?"

"My shoulder and head," she said hoarsely.

Off in the distance they could hear approaching sirens. Through the trees, they could also make out the fiery remains of the house trailer. Bolan unclipped his walkie-talkie again, but, as he'd feared, the dousing in the river had rendered it inoperable.

"Stay put," Bolan told her, rising to his feet. He withdrew his Beretta. "I'm going to try to catch up with the man who did this to you."

"But—"

"I don't think he's coming this way," Bolan assured her. "Just rest. You can call for help if I'm not back in a few minutes."

Bolan started off. "Thank you," Helena called out to him. As a bewildered afterthought, she added, "Who are you?"

Bolan vanished into the forest without answering. It didn't take him long to stray onto one of the established paths. He recognized the lay of the land and followed the path back toward the Gerley parking lot. The sirens were too loud for him to be able to discern any other sounds in the woods, and in the dark it was difficult for him to see if the other gunman had come this way.

Soon he'd come upon the hedges where he'd been doing his stakeout. Straying from the path, he headed through knee-high ferns into a meadow. There was enough moonlight on the clearing for him to see the tree where Don White had been conducting his surveillance. He broke into a run when he saw someone dangling upside down from one of the lower limbs.

Drawing closer, he realized it was White, who'd seemingly fallen from his post and accidentally wedged his ankle in the tree's crotch. The man's eyes were open but he wasn't moving, and there was a steady flow of blood streaming from his chest to the base of the tree. Bolan didn't need to get any closer to realize that the man had been shot.

Bolan reflexively ducked low and took cover behind the tree, wary that he'd be the next target. There was no further gunfire, however.

Cautiously moving out from behind the tree, the warrior reached up, dislodged White's foot and eased him to the ground. He checked for a pulse, but there wasn't one.

Moving away from the body, Bolan crouched and wandered back into the meadow. In the moonlight he was able to pinpoint the cluster of rocks where the classified papers had been found earlier that day. He approached the would-be drop site.

The papers were gone, which meant that White's killer was indeed involved in the espionage at Gerley Chemical.

Grim-faced, Bolan headed back to his slain companion.

2

Helena felt weak on her feet, her shoulder hurt and her skull throbbed with pain where her attacker had stuck her with his gun before pushing her from the bridge. Still, despite the stranger's advice, she didn't feel like remaining by the river indefinitely. She was wet and cold, and she wanted to get back to the trailer park so she could speak with the authorities.

When her rescuer didn't return after ten minutes, she set out on foot, moving slowly through the foliage as she sought out a path. She'd lost her shoes in the river, and every few steps she winced as a stone or some other object jabbed the soles of her feet. For protection she snatched up a fallen bough and clutched it like a baseball bat. She knew it wouldn't help her much if she was confronted by the gunman again, but having some sort of weapon, however primitive, made her feel less helpless.

There was a slight breeze in the air, and although she was already shuddering from the cold, Helena's flesh goose-bumped even more when the wind stirred up loose leaves or clattered tree limbs against one another.

To get back across the river she had to contend with the pedestrian bridge, and she let out a yelp halfway across when she inadvertently stepped on a jagged shard of glass from the shattered lamp. Clutching the railing for support, she fought back her tears and pried the sliver from her foot. Before going on, she paused and glanced down at the river that had nearly claimed her.

"Pull yourself together," she muttered. "You owe Joey that much."

She took a few deep breaths and rubbed her arms to fight off the chill. Once she'd brought herself under control, she crossed the bridge and headed up the incline to the trailer park.

TWO FIRE TRUCKS and three county sheriff's vehicles were on the scene. As firefighters hosed down the smoldering remains of the ravaged trailer, uniformed deputies held back a gathered crowd of onlookers.

"Come on, folks, let's call it a night, okay?" Deputy Todd Jeffler told the group. A former University of Michigan quarterback, Jeffler was an imposing presence even without the service revolver conspicuously displayed on his hip. As the last of the flames were extinguished behind him, the mob slowly began to break up and retreat. Jeffler continued to address the stragglers, but when he spotted Helena Simmons limping into view from the edge of the forest, he left crowd control to other officers and stepped over snarls of fire hoses until he reached her.

"Hey, you over there!" he said, frowning as he looked the woman over. "What happened to you?"

"It's a long story."

"Well, I got a feeling I'm gonna need to hear it," Jeffler told her. He motioned toward the nearest fire engine. "But first let's see if we can get you something to dry off with."

"Thanks."

They'd only taken a few steps when Jeffler heard a noise behind them. Glancing back, he saw Bolan emerging from the forest in his blacksuit, slipping his Beretta back into his holster. Jeffler pulled out his own gun and stepped in front of Helena.

"Hold it right there!" the deputy ordered.

Sheriff Mitch Hough, a tall, barrel-chested man in his mid-fifties, heard Jeffler and whipped out his gun as well, striding over to provide backup, drawling, "What do we have here?"

"I'm a federal agent," Bolan said, taking care to keep his hands out at his sides as he approached the others.

"It's okay, I know him," Helena told the officers. "He just saved my life."

Hough lowered his gun and motioned for Jeffler to do the same. When Bolan reached them, he pulled out a fake ID and handed it to Hough. "Mike Belasko," he said. "Special Agent, Justice Department."

In his line of work, Bolan often resorted to aliases, and Belasko was the most common. While it was true that he had indirect links to the Justice Department, in point of fact, Bolan's true affiliation was with Stony Man Farm, a classified installation in the Blue Ridge Mountains of Virginia. Along with a handful of other elite combat veterans based out of the secret compound, Bolan was called on to engage in those delicate missions that for various reasons fell beyond the scope of other agencies, or required tactics those same other agencies were wary of resorting to for fear of accountability. In short, Bolan's involvement meant a mission required results, sooner rather than later, and if that meant going at it with no holds barred, so be it.

"And what brings you to our little burg?" Hough asked as he handed the card back to Bolan. In the background, Deputy Jeffler went to the back of the fire truck to get a wool blanket.

"We have some classified business with Gerley Chemical on the other side of the woods." Bolan didn't bother to offer further details. At this point, no decision had been made whether to come public with the circumstances of Don White's death. Such a decision wasn't Bolan's concern anyway. That was a matter for those who'd been called in to tend to White's body and carry out the search for his killer. For now, Bolan's primary interest was in establishing the link between the trailer-home explosion and his foiled surveillance.

"I see." The sheriff turned to Helena. "What's this about him saving your life?"

Jeffler returned with the blanket. Helena thanked him and wrapped herself in it as she explained how she'd been surprised by a gunman shortly after the explosions and how Bolan had rescued her after she'd been shoved off the bridge into Long Noise river.

"Okay, fine," Hough said once she'd finished. "But now let's back up. What were you doing out here in the first place?"

Helena hesitated a moment, then glanced toward the collapsed shell of the house trailer. Firefighters were only now entering the structure to put out any spot blazes inside. "I was spying on the man who lives there. Ken Bridony."

"Why?" Jeffler asked.

Helena snapped. "Because I think he's the one who killed my brother and his family!"

While Jeffler exchanged glances with the sheriff, a pair of Bell helicopters warbled into view overhead, probing the night with the harsh glare of their searchlights.

"They're ours," Bolan told the officers as he eyed the choppers. Undoubtedly one of them was being commanded by Jack Grimaldi, Stony Man Farm's ace fly-boy and a friend of Bolan's dating back to his early clashes with the Mafia. Too much time had passed since White's murder, and Bolan doubted they were going to be able to find the agent's killer, but the situation called for a search.

"Go on," Sheriff Hough told Helena.

"Just give me a second, okay?" Helena pulled herself onto the back end of the nearest fire truck and drew her legs up so her feet would be covered by the blanket. One of the firemen produced a quart thermos and poured her a cup of coffee. She thanked the man and took a sip, then went on. "I'd been talking with my brother's neighbors, and they mentioned that two days before the murder he'd gotten into an argument with a handyman he'd hired to do some work at the farm. Joey'd ended up firing him, and the man apparently made some threats."

"And this man," Bolan guessed, "was Ken Bridony."

Helena nodded. "Anyway, I came by here earlier tonight to talk to some of the other people living here. I told them I was working on a magazine story about Halloween and just asked about Bridony in a roundabout way. I didn't want to arouse any suspicions not until I had more proof—"

"Ms. Simmons," Jeffler interrupted, "why didn't you just come to us?"

"I don't know. I should have, of course, but... he was my brother, don't you see?" Tears welled again in the woman's eyes. She clutched the blanket tightly around her and glared at the nearby trailer. Her voice cracked as she went on, "If this man killed him... killed Joey, his wife and his kids, I wanted to find out why. On my own."

Helena fell silent. None of the men wanted to push her any further, at least not at the moment. Bolan was particularly intrigued. Having no idea of the circumstances behind the apparent murder of Helena's brother and his family, he couldn't gauge if it might be in any way connected to the espionage at Gerley Chemical. But at some point he knew he'd have to find out more.

Sheriff Hough was finally about to resume questioning when three firemen grimly filed out of Bridony's house trailer. One of them made a beeline to the deputies.

"You find out what started it?" Jeffler asked.

The fireman nodded. "Back bedroom was filled with gas cans and Molotov cocktails."

"For Devil's Night?" the deputy queried.

"Beats me," the fireman replied, "and you're not going to have much luck asking the guy we found in there."

"You found someone?"

"Yep. Or at least what's left of him. Gonna need dental records before you can fill out the toe tag on his body bag."

"I don't believe it," Helena gasped. "I mean, I just assumed the man who attacked me was Bridony. But if it wasn't Bridony, then who was it?"

ROSEY TOSCA HAD BEEN a Canadian track and football star ten years ago at East Windsor High, and he was still in peak condition thanks to a steady workout regimen. So it wasn't surprising that he'd been able to kill Don White, make a quick snatch at the Gerley drop site, and still slip back through the woods to safety before the authorities had a chance to lay their dragnet in hopes of apprehending him.

Now, catching his breath in the back seat of a taxi headed south on Woodward Avenue, the twenty-seven-year-old indulged himself with his daily cigarette, one of those classy Cartiers that came in oblong packs. He lighted up and drew in a deep breath, welcoming the hot sting of smoke bounding off the base of his lungs. He exhaled slowly, pursing his lips to blow a narrow cloud of smoke at the meter mounted behind the front seat.

"Ah, excuse me, sir," the driver said, glancing at Tosca in the rearview mirror. "But this is a no smokin' cab."

"That so?" Tosca peeled a ten-dollar bill from his money clip and folded it neatly in half before passing it up to the driver. "Andrew Jackson here says it's all right."

"Aw, well, hell..." The driver flashed a gap-toothed smile as he spied the denomination. "Who am I to argue with the President?"

"That's more like it."

"You just puff away," the driver said as the traffic light changed and he crossed Long Lake Road. "Only could you maybe not blow smoke up here? See, I'm tryin' to quit, but when I get a whiff of that...mmm boy, I get a real bad hankerin', know what I mean?"

"Yeah," Tosca agreed. "Sometimes it's tough to kick bad habits."

Tosca knew all about bad habits. This night alone he'd been a party to murder, arson, kidnapping, aggravated assault and espionage, and if he hadn't encountered the other gunman in the woods near the trailer park, he would have added rape to the list.

The taxi was now heading through Bloomfield Hills, one of Detroit's more exclusive suburbs, and as they left Woodward Avenue and headed down a series of side streets, Tosca admired the lavish estates around him. He'd been inside a few of them, sometimes at the owners' invitation, other times at his own. Over there on his right was a mansion where he'd nibbled caviar and swilled champagne with an auto executive after a million-dollar cocaine transaction. And up the block was a servants' quarters he'd broken into a few weeks ago, raping a house maid for three hours and afterward swearing her to silence with a vow to kill her children if she talked. He smiled as he recalled the look of horror on the woman's face when he'd yanked her parakeet from its cage and twisted its head off as a way of showing her he meant business.

Two blocks later, Tosca stubbed out his cigarette and told the driver to pull over in front of a small residential park.

"Eight-fifty," the cabbie said.

Tosca handed the man another ten-dollar bill and told him to keep the change. The cabbie thanked him and drove off, leaving Tosca at the curb.

The hardman cracked his knuckles and was about to cross the street when he spotted a middle-aged woman out walking her dog. When she passed under a streetlight, Tosca saw that she was quite a looker. He grinned as he played out a possible scenario. She was bundled up with her hands stuffed inside her coat, so there was always a chance she was carrying Mace, but he doubted it. The dog might put up a fuss, but it was small enough that a well-placed kick would nullify that threat. And there were plenty of bushes in the park. Glancing at his watch, he figured he could drag her off, have his way with her, make sure she couldn't cause problems for him later, and still have time to make his rendezvous with the big man. It was tempting, especially since he'd been thwarted from getting his rocks off earlier.

There was a bus stop in front of the park. Tosca took a few steps to his right and sat on the curbside bench next to the route sign, doing his best to look like he was waiting for the next bus.

"Come to daddy," he murmured, watching the woman out of the corner of his eye. "That's a good girl...."

Before she reached the park, however, the woman suddenly detoured, heading up the front walk of a two-story brownstone bathed in the yellow glow of security lights. The front door opened and a man stepped out onto the porch, calling out to the woman. She unclipped the dog's leash and the animal bounded up the steps into the man's waiting embrace. He picked the dog up, giving it a hug, then leaned forward and kissed the woman as she stepped up onto the porch.

"It's your lucky night, bitch," Tosca muttered.

He waited a couple minutes, then rose from the bench and backtracked another six blocks until he reached a cul-de-sac bumping up against the twelfth hole at the Pontiac Meadows Country Club. There were six huge houses resting on pie-slice lots, all of them surrounded by tall walls and fences as well as security gates across their driveways.

Tosca went up to one of the security gates and planted his thumb on a buzzer built into the adjacent brick wall. Through the gate he could see a camera aimed at him. He eyed the lens with cool detachment. A moment passed before a burst of static squawked from the small speaker mounted below the buzzer, followed by a man's voice.

"Yes, who is it?"

"The Tooth Fairy," Tosca retorted. "C'mon, give me a break and look in your goddamn monitor."

There was a pause before the disembodied voice responded. "Wait right there."

"I'd rather come in," Tosca said. "Y'know, maybe have a little drink or something."

No answer. The hardman glared at the speaker, fighting back his temper. Did he ever hate dealing with these self-important sons of bitches. If you saw one of them at his office, the goddamn secretary would stick you in a goddamn waiting room for half an hour. Call one on the phone and you were put on hold. Not because he was busy with something else, mind you. It was just one of the little power-trip mind games to try to make you feel like you weren't important enough for the man to drop what he was doing.

A door opened in the enclosed walkway linking the garage to the main house. Out stepped a hulking man of six-three, his two hundred and twenty-six pounds straining against the fabric of a sharkskin suit. Frankie Cerdae, the big man's bodyguard. Flat nose, scruffy mustache, small dark eyes always filled with a menacing gleam. He walked with a lumbering gait, shoulders rolling slightly with each step. Tosca figured the man was packing a .44 Magnum inside his coat, possibly a smaller automatic tucked behind his back. Tosca didn't fear many people in this world, but Cerdae was one of them.

Not that he was about to let Cerdae know that.

"Hey, Tubby," Tosca called out casually as Cerdae ambled up to the gate. "Open up already."

"Fuck you," Cerdae boomed in his loud baritone voice as he held out his right hand. "Did you get it?"

"What do you think? Of course I got it."

"Well, let's have it!" Cerdae growled impatiently. "I don't have all night."

"Where's my money?"

"Holy shit, do we have to play this same fucking game every time you pick up a drop?" Cerdae snapped his fingers and held his outstretched palm closer to the gate. "You hand over the drop first, *then* you get paid. Understand?"

"How about this time I bring it in and give it to the boss myself?"

"No dice," Cerdae said. "He's busy."

"Yeah, yeah."

"He's busy!" The bodyguard reached in his coat pocket and pulled out an inch-thick envelope, letting Tosca have a good look at it. "Here, you want this or not?"

Tosca eyed the envelope. Fifteen grand for one night's work.

"All right, all right." He opened his own coat and pulled out the container with the papers from Gerley Chemical. He thrust it through the gate's bars. Cerdae took it in exchange for the envelope.

"Good," the bodyguard said. "Now beat it."

Tosca sneered at the bigger man. "Hey, nice seeing you, too, Tubby!"

Cerdae turned and headed back up the walk. Tosca stared at him, fury boiling in his chest. Goddamn ingrates, he thought to himself. Hanging out in their goddamn castles while the grunts took all the risks.

"One of these days," Tosca whispered under his breath. He walked away from the mansion, breaking his personal code and tapping out a second cigarette. "One of these days..."

3

"It happened a little over a month ago," Helena explained. "We have an old family farm just outside of Pontiac. My brother had been living there the past year along with Ruby and the two kids. They were really fixing the place up, too. New barn, new fences, and they'd redecorated most of the house, too. The plan was to have everything finished by Christmas. But, then . . ."

Helena's voice trailed off and her eyes misted. "I'm sorry."

"That's all right."

When Bolan had requested a chance to ask her a few questions, Helena had invited Bolan to her Talville Terrace apartment, three miles from the trailer park. They were sitting at the kitchen table, which had a window view of the Detroit skyline, still smeared with clouds of smoke left in the wake of Devil's Night. Helena had changed into dry clothes and pulled her hair back into a ponytail. She wasn't wearing makeup, and her cheekbone was still discolored and swollen where her assailant had struck her, but despite her ordeal, or perhaps because of it, she radiated an aura of resilience. Tears aside, she was a survivor.

"Ken Bridony," Bolan asked, "was hired to do some work on the farm?"

"Yes. At least that's what I've been told. He was primarily a carpenter, but he also did some plumbing and electrical work. From what I hear, it was the job he did wiring the barn that got him fired. Joey said it wasn't up to code, and he wanted it redone. Ken said he wouldn't unless he was paid extra. Joey said no way." Helena blushed a moment, then went on, "Well, from what I understand, Joey didn't use quite those words, but it was pretty clear that he didn't want Ken around anymore. He paid him a whole week's salary but fired him on the spot."

A teakettle whistled to life on the stove. Helena excused herself to tend to it, asking Bolan, "Would you like some tea?"

Bolan shook his head. He felt a little callous putting Helena through questioning at a time like this, but he felt it was necessary to get a clear picture of what had happened at the Simmons farm, especially now that it appeared to have some bearing on the espionage at Gerley Chemical. He gave Helena a moment to regain her composure, then asked, "The murders took place the weekend after Bridony was fired?"

"Yes." Helena dropped a teabag into her cup and filled it with boiling water. Her voice took on a hardened edge. "They were killed with shotgun blasts at close range. Joey and Ruby were found outside, near the corral. The kids..." A lone tear spilled out the corner of one eye and trickled down her cheek. She wiped it away. "The kids were in their beds. The coroner said they were asleep when it happened."

On the kitchen counter Bolan saw a photo portrait of Joey Simmons and his family. Provided it was recent, the two children looked like they were both under five years old. Any kind of murder was reprehensible, but to Bolan the thought of innocent children being killed seemed particularly heinous. He could understand Helena's desire to help catch the man responsible, the need to find out why the killings had occurred in the first place. He wanted to help, as much for her sake as his. The best he could do for the moment, however, was to offer his sympathies.

"I'm sorry," he told her again.

"Thanks." Helena paced the kitchen, waiting for the tea to steep. "The police weren't able to come up with any solid suspects, and when I found out about Bridony and realized they hadn't even heard about the argument, much less brought him in for questioning, I decided to take matters into my own hands. It's not like I didn't have any experience...."

"I can see that," Bolan said, shifting his gaze to the wall of the nearby living room, which was lined with framed covers of *Detroit Monthly* magazine. "You're a reporter?"

"I'm one of the editors, actually, but I also do some investigative pieces."

The phone suddenly clanged to life in the dining room.

"Speak of the devil," Helena said as she went to answer it. "It's my business line. Would you excuse me?"

"Sure."

Bolan left the kitchen and glanced over the magazine covers. Most of them featured local celebrities, but there were a few covers devoted to other topics, and in each instance Helena had the byline for the featured story. One was on street gangs and the crack epidemic, another on safety violations at several auto-manufacturing plants. But what riveted Bolan's attention most was a cover graced by an aerial photo of Gerley Chemical's Talville plant, along with a headline that read WHAT PRICE GERLEY? The smaller print credited the in-depth story to none other than Helena Simmons. Bolan checked for a date and saw that it was the August issue.

There was a bookcase on the opposite wall, and as he expected, Bolan found back issues of the monthly stored in boxed sets. He pulled out the August issue and began skimming through Helena's article, which focused on Gerley's biochemical research contracts with the Defense Department. Ironically, while Helena's primary editorial slant dealt with the moral issue of Gerley's involvement in what was essentially an outlawed form of weaponry, she also raised questions about the fear that research results and test materials might become the target of foreign agents. She'd even gone so far as to outline possible scenarios by which such agents might get their hands on such items. Remarkably some of her prophecies had since come to pass, although Bolan doubted that Helena was even aware of it because the incidents were all classified.

Bolan looked across the room at Helena, debating whether to divulge to her that part of his present mission dealt with the security breaches at Gerley. He decided against it. If she was anything like other crack investigators Bolan had dealt with in the past, there would be no way he could pick her brains for information without rousing her suspicions. And once you opened the Pandora's box of a reporter's suspicions, Bolan knew there was no way to close it. He figured whatever information he might gain would come at the price of drawing her into the investigation, and for her sake as well as his he didn't want to see that happen.

Helena had her back turned to him, but once she hung up the phone she turned around and he could see the troubled expression on her face.

"That was one of our writers from the city desk," she told him. "He was at the sheriff's station checking the blotter. He heard they just finished searching the rest of Bridony's trailer. They found a shotgun, same gauge as the one used on Joey's family."

"You're not surprised, are you?" Bolan asked.

"No, I guess not, but . . ." Helena paused to sip her tea.

Bolan guessed what she was thinking. "But you don't think the shotgun really belongs to Bridony."

"No," she agreed. "I think it was planted there, along with all the gasoline and Molotov cocktails."

"Someone was trying to frame him."

Helena finished her tea and set the cup back on its saucer. "You know," she confessed, "when I went to that trailer park tonight, I was positive Ken Bridony killed my brother. Now I'm almost as positive he didn't."

"And you think it was the man you surprised outside the trailer."

Helena looked hard at Bolan. "Don't you?"

"LINE UP, LADIES, the Stud has arrived!"

Rosey Tosca dismounted his chrome-encrusted Harley and grinned widely at the assorted women in denim and black leather idling with their boyfriends outside Mofo's, a ramshackle biker's bar located in the heart of Macomb County, a good half-hour drive from downtown Detroit. There were at least two dozen other low-slung, high-powered motorcycles parked outside, and most of the owners were members of the Renegades, the most feared biker gang within a fifty-mile radius of Motor City.

One of the gang members flipped his middle finger in the air and snarled, "Up yours, Rosey!"

"No thanks, Brewster." Tosca laughed off the taunt, focusing his attention on the biker's woman, who was amply proportioned with henna-dyed hair and a thick layer of makeup that obscured her age. She might have been sixteen or thirty-six; in the dim light outside the bar it was hard to tell. Tosca winked at her. "Now, if you want to tell me 'Up yours,' I might be interested."

"Fat chance," the woman said, smacking her bubble gum.

"Your loss, doll."

"Don't push your luck, Tosca," Brewster warned him.

"Hey, you should be flattered, asshole." Tosca lightly punched the biker's shoulder, then pulled his arm back before Brewster could grab it. Blowing a kiss at the woman, he said, "If you change your mind, I'll be inside."

As the hardman bounded up the steps leading to the bar, Brewster eyed his fellow gang members and pleaded, "Why do I have to put up with that fucker's lip every time he comes here, huh? Why can't we just chop him up and throw him on the barbecue or something?"

"Bitch, bitch, bitch," another of the bikers gibed. "Hey, Brewster, grab another beer and shut up!"

Tosca wasn't concerned about Brewster's threats or any of the other ribbings he invariably received when he showed up at Mofo's, which was usually a couple times a week. He knew he was protected by mandate of Scotty Sear, leader of the Renegades, and for good reason. After all, it was Tosca who kept the Renegades in a steady supply of cocaine, crack and heroin, not only for private consumption but also for peddling on the streets. If that wasn't incentive enough, there were rumors that Tosca's drug operations were somehow linked to the Bariggia organized crime family. The Renegades had their own ties with the Mob, and they didn't want to foul up their relationship by manhandling a mutual ally.

So Tosca strolled into Mofo's with an air of impunity, drinking in the heady smell of smoke, beer and vomit. A jukebox in the corner was blaring and the bar was crowded, especially when one considered it was three in the morning. Most of the action was around the pool tables, where a couple of high-stakes games were in progress. Tosca leaned against the bar and ordered a draft from a dull-eyed bartender who was easily the largest man in the room. Once he had his beer, Tosca wandered over to the nearest table.

Scotty Sear, a tall, muscular man with pale blue eyes and a black widow tattooed on his left cheek, was in the process of running stripes off the table, barely taking time to line up his shots. His aim was deadly, and each time he pumped his cue stick, balls thunked into pockets like a steady fall of rain. The other bikers cheered him on, and soon the game was over.

Sear smugly set his cue aside and snatched up the crumpled fifty-dollar bill his opponent had tossed onto the table. He nonchalantly unfolded the bill, then slipped it down the prominent cleavage of a buxom brunette standing beside him. "Here, now you can get your nails done tomorrow."

The woman tilted her head back and laughed. Sear drew the woman close and kissed her, letting his hand stray down her backside. She rubbed up close to him, raising one leg to stroke Sear's groin with her inner thigh. As she was doing so, she spotted Tosca standing a few feet away, watching her.

"Rosey!" she cried out happily, pulling away from Sear and offering Tosca an inviting smile. Sear couldn't help but notice, but it didn't seem to bother him.

"Nice piece of shooting, Scotty," Tosca told the gang leader, raising his voice to be heard above the surrounding pandemonium.

"Hell, I've done better."

"Haven't we all . . ."

"Maybe so," Scotty said, taking a cigarette pack from his coat pocket and shaking a few loose. "Tell me, Rosey, what's the weather forecast?"

Tosca waved away the cigarettes but clicked his lighter and held it out to Scotty's woman. She took one of the cigarettes and smiled as Tosca lighted her up. Even as she was making eyes at Tosca, she was wrapping her arm around Sear. Tosca could feel pangs of arousal. He knew from experience that the woman liked getting it on with two guys at the same time, and both he and Scotty liked the arrangement as well.

"The weather?" Tosca repeated, smiling at both Scotty and the woman. "I see snow, snow and more snow."

"Yeah?" Scotty smiled. Snow, snow and more snow . . . That meant three kilos of uncut coke. Very nice. Very nice indeed. "If we get that much, we just might have to break out the snow shovels." He was talking about distribution, which would probably mean cutting a deal with some downtown street gangs.

"I'm looking at tomorrow afternoon," Tosca told him.

"Same place?" Scotty asked.

"Same place."

"Sounds good, but lemme make a quick phone call to line up the shovels," Scotty said, fishing through his coat for a quarter. He pried the woman's hand from his side and told her, "Keep Rosey company, Jeri, okay?"

"Sure thing," she said, transferring her hand to Rosey's shoulder.

Tosca and Jeri watched Sear elbow his way through his fellow bikers to a pay phone mounted on the wall next to the men's room. Tosca's eyes were still on the gang leader when he felt Jeri's lips closing around his earlobe. "Hey, baby," she whispered. "You got some candy for me?"

"Maybe."

"Oh, sure you do, baby." Jeri eased her tongue out between her lips and licked at Tosca's ear as her hand drifted down his side, passing over the .357 Magnum tucked inside his waistband and settling on his groin. "You know what Jeri likes," she moaned in his ear. "Just like Jeri knows what you like."

"Well, that's not where I keep my candy, sweet-cakes," Tosca told her. "You know that."

"Uh-huh." Jeri brought her hand up and began searching through Tosca's pockets. He turned his head, meeting her lips with his own. As they kissed, he could feel her fingers inside his coat, closing around two glass vials of cocaine. One was meant as a sampler for Sear, but the other was all Jeri's.

"Just the one, sweetcakes," he reminded her. "Trust me, it'll be plenty."

"Oooh, it's that good, huh?"

"There's one way to find out," he told her.

She kissed him hard, stabbing her tongue deep into his mouth, then suddenly pulled away, withdrawing her hand from his coat. "I'll be right back," she assured him, closing her fist around the glass vial. "I just need to powder my nose."

Tosca grinned at her, then drained the last of his beer and held it out until the bartender snatched it away, replacing it with another. Tosca paid for the drink, tripping the tender generously, then turned back to bask in the boisterous pandemonium around him. There was an argument taking place at one of the tables, and in one of the booths a woman was straddling a biker, her skirt hiked up around her thighs and her head tilted back as she swayed back and forth in the man's lap.

Now this was living, he thought to himself happily. None of the highbrow pretensions he had to put up with when he did business in Dearborn or Bloomfield Hills. Here he felt he was amid kindred spirits, people who knew how to seize the moment and milk it for all it was worth.

Tosca was so carried away with his reverie that he didn't notice Deputy Todd Jeffler making his way through the crowd toward him. Jeffler was out of uniform, wearing a brown leather jacket and black denim slacks, but he still drew his share of stares. He didn't have to flash his badge to get Tosca's attention, either.

"Outside," Jeffler told Tosca once they were standing face-to-face. "Now!"

"I haven't finished my beer," Tosca told the officer.

Jeffler grabbed the glass from the hardman's hand and threw it across the room, smashing it against the wall. "Now you have."

Tosca sighed and started to follow the deputy out of the bar. He offered a grin to several bikers at the nearest pool table. Gesturing at Jeffler, he chuckled. "You'll have to excuse him. It's that time of the month."

Instead of using the main entrance, Jeffler escorted Tosca out the side door, which led to a cramped, dim-lit alley. The air was foul with a week's worth of garbage spilling from the top of an overfilled Dumpster.

As he followed Jeffler down the steps, Tosca drawled, "Okay, okay, what's the big—"

He was taken by surprise when a hulking figure suddenly lunged from the shadows, grabbing him by the lapels of his jacket and slamming him into the Dumpster.

"Hey!" Tosca roared at Frankie Cerdae. "What's the big idea?"

"What do you think, you little shit?" Cerdae raged. "Did you really think we wouldn't find out?"

"Find out what?" Tosca asked, appealing to Jeffler. "What's he talking about?"

"He's talking about some unfinished business, Rosey," Jeffler explained.

"You didn't tell us there was a witness who saw you leaving Bridony's trailer tonight," Cerdae growled, getting to the bottom line.

"Witness? Are you kidding? She didn't see squat! I was wearing a mask."

"Why didn't you get rid of her?" Cerdae demanded.

"Hey, I was going to, but I got interrupted, okay?" Tosca wrangled his way out of the bigger man's grip and moved away from the Dumpster. "Look, it's nothing to get bent over. It was just some woman."

"Oh yeah?" Jeffler said. "Well, that 'just some woman' happens to be Helena Simmons. Does that ring a bell, Rosey?"

"What?" Tosca couldn't believe his ears. "Simmons? Come on, man, you got to be kidding."

"Hey," the deputy said, "I was there when she showed up. Maybe she didn't get a good look at you, but give her half a chance and she's going to start piecing things together. And we can't have that, can we?''

When Tosca hesitated, Cerdae moved in again, this time pulling out his Magnum and putting the barrel to Rosey's chin. He repeated Jeffler's threat. "And we can't have that, can we?''

"No. But don't worry. I'll take care of her."

"When?" Cerdae wanted to know.

"First thing tomorrow," Tosca promised. "You have my word."

"Your word," Jeffler scoffed. "That and two bucks'll buy you a beer at this dump."

"I'm telling you," Tosca said, "the broad's as good as dead."

Cerdae smiled and stepped back from Tosca. "That's what we like to hear." Abruptly the man's smile turned to a savage scowl. "We'll keep our eyes on the obituary page. If her name isn't there tomorrow night, yours will the day after."

Jeffler and Cerdae turned and walked down the alley, disappearing around the corner once they reached the back parking lot. Tosca remained near the Dumpster, fighting to contain his growing rage. A part of him was tempted to follow the men and gun them down with his .357. It wouldn't be the first time men had died in the parking lot of Mofo's, and it sure as hell wouldn't be the last.

But, of course, Jeffler and Cerdae were only errand boys. Icing them would create more problems than it would solve, and Tosca knew it. No, when he weighed the situation, his course was clear. Helena Simmons had to die.

Tosca bent over, raising one cuff of his pants high enough that he could reach inside his cowboy boot. He pulled out the envelope he'd received from Cerdae earlier that evening. He counted out ten thousand dollars, then slipped it back down his boot. He stuffed the other four grand into the envelope.

Whistling nonchalantly, Tosca swaggered out to the front of Mofo's, where a handful of bikers were still anchored to their Harleys. He tracked down Brewster, who was sitting by himself.

"What the fuck do you want?" the biker asked as Tosca approached him.

"Got a peace offering for you," the hardman said, handing over the envelope. "Go ahead, open it."

Brewster opened the envelope and peered in. He let out a low whistle, then raised his gaze to Tosca. "Lotta money," he said, adding sarcastically, "What do I gotta do, kill somebody?"

Tosca smiled. "Smart boy..."

4

It was shortly after dawn at the Macomb County Sheriff's Department. Crowded into Hough's nondescript office were the sheriff, Deputy Jeffler, Mack Bolan and plainclothes detective Keith Tabell. The latter had just joined the briefing, bringing in a foam cup filled with black coffee.

"Well, the dental charts matched up," Tabell reported as he leaned against a nearby file cabinet. "The dead guy was definitely Ken Bridony. And what's more, the coroner says he was dead before his trailer caught on fire. Blunt trauma to the back of the skull."

"No real surprise there," Bolan said. "But what we still have to find out is who wanted him framed for the Simmons murders, and why."

"The 'why' part seems pretty obvious," Hough speculated. "Given that argument Bridony had with Joey Simmons after he was fired, there's a clear-cut motive. Provided nobody shows up offering an alibi for Bridony being somewhere else at the time of the killings, it'd be easy enough to make a case for opportunity. He's a perfect fall guy."

Tabell added, "Especially now that he's dead and not able to defend himself."

"Exactly," Bolan said. "And that's what bothers me. Whoever the real killer is, he went out of his way to try to point the finger at Bridony. First, he had to know about the argument, then he had to plant the shotgun and all those incendiary devices at the trailer."

Hough picked up on Bolan's train of thought. "So you're saying the Simmonses weren't victims of random violence."

"Yeah," Bolan said. "If that was the case, the killer'd just hit and run. Odds are he'd be halfway across the country now. And also there's no record of anything being taken from the farm, is there?"

"Negative," Detective Tabell replied, skimming over his notes. "So unless we missed something, that rules out robbery."

"I think you guys are all overlooking something," Deputy Jeffler put in. "Maybe Bridony *did* kill the Simmones, only he had an accomplice, and that's who killed him and started the fire."

"Possibly," Tabell said, "but that still leaves us at square one."

"Maybe not," Sheriff Hough said, tapping a pencil on his desk. "Maybe not."

"What do you mean?" Bolan asked.

Hough rose from his chair and went over to the file cabinet, motioning for Tabell to move aside so he could open the top drawer. As he sifted through files, he told Bolan, "Over the past four months or so, we've had a string of disappearances. Teenage boys for the most part, usually runaways, but also a couple instances of those kids you find selling flowers at street corners. Ah, here we go.''

''What's the connection?'' Bolan asked.

''The connection,'' Hough replied, ''is that we brought Bridony in for questioning on the disappearances at one point. Apparently somebody'd seen him buying flowers from one of the kids an hour before he was reported missing. We couldn't pin anything on him, though. Tried surveillance for a few days and came up empty-handed, too, so we wrote him off.''

''Which isn't to say he wasn't guilty,'' Jeffler pointed out. ''Maybe he *did* pick up one of those kids and used him for an accomplice, then maybe the kid turned against him.''

As the others continued to discuss the possibilities, Bolan listened silently, trying to keep things in focus. It was maddening that every time he seemed on the verge of piecing together the puzzle of the espionage at Gerley Chemical, another puzzle was added to the mix. Now instead of looking into the mere stealing of government secrets, it seemed that he also had to be concerned about an unsolved mass murder and the mysterious disappearance of local teenage boys. He had no idea how it all fit together, or even if it, in fact, did.

For now, though, it seemed that Bolan's best bet was to pursue a solution to the mass murders. Because of the top-secret nature of the Gerley Chemical investigation, he wasn't at liberty to discuss strategy with anyone in the room, and, in all honesty, he had his doubts about the validity of a "missing teenager" connection. Although he hadn't been able to get a look at the man who'd abducted Helena at the trailer park, Bolan had heard him speak and gotten a decent look at his physique. There was no way it could have been an adolescent.

The warrior turned to the sheriff. "Did anything noteworthy turn up in the autopsies?"

"Autopsies?" Hough queried.

"Most likely they'd list the angle of entry of the shotgun blasts," Bolan said. "We might be able to figure out if we're looking for someone right-handed or—"

"No, you don't understand, Mr. Belasko," the sheriff interjected. "There weren't any autopsies."

"No?" Bolan frowned. "Why not?"

"Family wanted it that way. Besides, it was pretty clear how they all died."

"That's not the only reason you do an autopsy. I—"

"Mr. Belasko," Hough interrupted again, this time with growing irritation, "I don't need a lecture on criminal procedure, thank you very much. Yes, of course there was a chance autopsies could have turned up the kind of details you mentioned, but it was a long shot. You know that. We weighed the benefits, and the bottom line was we just didn't think the situation warranted overriding the family's desires."

"By the family, are we talking about Helena?" Bolan asked.

Hough shook his head. "No, she was all for it. But her parents were just as adamantly opposed. We went with them. Judgment call."

"Well, you made a mistake."

"You're entitled to your opinion, Mr. Belasko," Hough responded. "But I would remind you that this is my jurisdiction, and I'd thank you to get off your high horse and quit talking down to us country folks like we were just born yesterday."

"I hear you," Bolan said, rising from his chair. "Loud and clear. If you'll excuse me, I think you can carry on here without my help."

"I'll show you out," Deputy Jeffler offered, beating Bolan to the door.

"I know the way."

"It's okay. My shift's over anyway." Jeffler followed the Executioner into the hallway. Once they'd closed the door behind them, the deputy fell in step beside Bolan.

"Look, Belasko," he went on, "I have to apologize for the boss. He's been a little on edge the past few weeks. As you can expect, folks around here are all up in arms over the killings and the missing kids. They want something done, and so does the sheriff. You have to believe that."

"I know he means well, but I have to question his methods."

At the end of the hallway, Jeffler held the door open for Bolan. They headed out together to the parking lot.

"What do you intend to do now?" the deputy asked.

"I'm going to get together with Helena and go have a talk with her parents. I'm sure they want to see the killers brought to justice, and if they understand the importance of doing autopsies, maybe they'll change their minds."

"Well, I doubt it," Jeffler said, "but I wish you luck."

"Thanks."

Bolan got into his rental car and pulled out into the early-morning rush hour. Jeffler headed to his Dodge pickup, slamming his fist on the dashboard as he climbed behind the wheel. He was concerned about the federal agent's continued presence in Talville, particularly when he was spending so much time with Helena. Either one of them posed a potential threat; together it seemed even more possible that they might stumble on enough evidence to blow the lid off the clandestine activities to which Jeffler was a party. He wasn't about to let that happen.

He grabbed the cellular phone under his dashboard. He knew Tosca's number by heart and quickly dialed it. Tosca answered on the fifth ring.

"It's Jeffler," he whispered urgently into the receiver. "We've got more problems."

"Well, give me a chance to take care of the ones I already got, would you?" the hardman retorted.

"They want to dig up the bodies."

"Who?" Tosca demanded. "Who wants to dig up the bodies?"

"Belasko," Jeffler reported. "The guy you ran into on the bridge. He's pushing to have the whole family exhumed for autopsies."

"Shit!"

"Shit is right. If they do any kind of detailed tissue studies, everything could start to unravel."

"You don't have to tell me that."

"Then we need to act," Jeffler said. "Now!"

"I hear you."

"Belasko's planning to take Helena to her folks and try to get them to approve the autopsies. It'll be a perfect chance to take them out."

"I'll take care of it," Tosca said. "What about the bodies?"

"Let me worry about that."

"No!"

"Why not?" the deputy asked. "I know how to get to the—"

"Look," Tosca interrupted. "I'll handle that, too."

"But it needs to be done right away, and if you're taking care of—"

"I said I'll handle it! You just keep your cool and stay on top of your end of things. Don't forget, you've got to round up all that shit on the Bolivian's shopping list by tonight."

"I know," Jeffler said. "But I—"

"You just handle that and leave the rest to me," Tosca said. "I'll see you at the warehouse tonight."

He hung up before Jeffler could say anything else.

As he slowly set down the receiver, the deputy drew in a deep breath, trying to slow the jackhammer pounding of his heart. Until last night it had seemed as if they were going to get away with everything. But now it all was closing in on him.

"Hey, Todd buddy!"

Startled, Jeffler glanced up and saw another deputy standing outside his truck. How long had he been there?

"You all right, man?" the deputy asked as Jeffler rolled down his window.

"Yeah, yeah. I'm fine," Jeffler lied.

"Well, you look like death warmed over. Good thing it's your day off. You need to crawl under the covers and forget about things for a while."

"Ain't that the fucking truth," Jeffler mumbled as he keyed the ignition. Of course, he knew that he wouldn't be getting any rest today. Not by a long shot.

ROSEY TOSCA WAS equally unnerved by the prospect of the Simmons family being exhumed. As he hung up the phone after speaking to Jeffler, he rummaged through the pockets of the coat slung over the chair beside him, taking out his cigarettes. There was no way he was going to get through the day on just one.

He was in the living room of his modest home near Ridon, a crowded suburban development heavily populated with working-class Italians. Although he spent a considerable amount of time living out of high-priced hotels, Tosca preferred to keep a lower profile in terms of his listed residence. It was partly a ploy to defer any possible suspicions about his source of income, but he was also fond of the neighborhood, with its boisterous children, roaming odors of fine Italian cooking, and an old-world camaraderie.

As Tosca lighted his cigarette, Scotty Sear ambled in from the adjacent bedroom, zipping up his jeans. Through the open doorway, the hardman saw Jeri dozing amid disheveled sheets and blankets, sated and spent from her hours of passion shared with her lovers.

"You look like shit, man," Sear commented as he helped himself to one of Tosca's cigarettes. "Bad news on the phone?"

"Yeah. Got ourselves a problem."

"I heard something about bodies."

Tosca nodded. "Simmons family. Looks like they're gonna be dug up for an autopsy."

The biker inhaled a lungful of smoke and blew it out in one harsh blast. "When?"

"Soon as they can pull all the right strings. Probably this afternoon at the earliest."

Sear checked a wall clock. "Leaves me a couple hours."

"You want to take care of it?" Tosca asked.

"Yeah, hell, why not? I'll just swing by the house and grab a couple of the guys. You need to line up that coke shipment, right?"

Tosca nodded. "Right."

"We better arrange a different pickup spot, too," Sear said. "Cemetery's apt to be a little too hot now."

"Yeah. Tell you what. If you can take care of the bodies, I'll handle the shipment myself and bring it to the compound. Okay?"

"Deal." Sear pulled on a T-Shirt and jabbed his arms into the sleeves of his leather jacket. "And we'll have to dismantle the lab, too, at least until the heat dies down at the boneyard."

"Good idea."

"Later," Sear said on his way out the door.

Tosca took another long drag on his cigarette. Once he heard Sear's bike rev, he picked up the phone and put through a quick call to John Brewster, rousing the biker from bed.

"Showtime," Tosca said into the phone.

"Huh? What?" Brewster mumbled groggily. "Hey, man, it's still nighttime!"

"It's morning, asshole. Shut up and listen!"

Tosca replayed Jeffler's news about the federal agent and Helena Simmons heading out to see the woman's parents, and quickly sketched out a plan for Brewster to carry out. He had the man repeat everything to make sure he had it straight.

"Good," Tosca said once Brewster had recited the information verbatim. "Now get cracking!"

"Listen," the biker said. "Any objection if I bring along some backup?"

"Who you got in mind?"

"This kid's been hounding me to get in the gang. He'd be perfect...and I won't have to cut him in on the money."

"I don't care if you use your mother, as long as you get the job done and do it right," Tosca told him. "Remember, fuck up and you're on your own."

Tosca hung up the phone and smiled to himself as he straggled into his kitchen. He couldn't believe how easy it'd been to delegate the dirty work. Hell, he might as well be running the Renegades himself.

He yawned as he raided the refrigerator for a quart container of orange juice. He leaned against the sink and sipped the juice as he stared out the window at his backyard, where his five attack-trained Dobermans were frolicking across the leaf-covered lawn. When a garbage truck rolled past the brick wall separating his yard from a back alley, the dogs suddenly turned heel and barked their way to the gate, where they continued to hound the garbageman as he collected Tosca's trash.

"Morning, big shot," Jeri purred as she wandered in from the side hallway, wearing only one of Tosca's T-shirts. "Where's Scotty?"

"Had some errands to run."

"Hmm, then it's just you and me, yes?" Jeri nuzzled up close to Tosca, wiping juice from his lips with her finger. "Come back to bed...."

"No can do. I got a big day ahead of me."

"Please," the woman pleaded. She pulled the T-shirt up, giving Tosca a good look at her body. "I need some more of what you got."

"Maybe later." He opened a cupboard and took down a mason jar filled with amphetamines. He swallowed a couple and stashed a handful in his pants pocket, then held out the jar to Jeri. "Here, have some breakfast, then get your clothes on. Five minutes and we're outta here."

Jeri took some of the pills and headed off to get dressed. Tosca splashed cold water on his face, then toweled himself off and wandered into the bedroom, throwing on a shirt and a pair of lizard-skin boots. Jeri watched him as he took his gun off the dresser and inspected it.

"You ever killed anybody, Rosey?"

"Nobody that didn't have it coming to them," he replied, slipping the gun inside the waistband of his pants.

"C'mon, I'm serious," she said. "Did you?"

Tosca smiled and shook his head. "Of course not. Me, I'm a regular Boy Scout. I just carry this around for self-defense."

Jeri laughed as she pulled on her Levi's. "If you're a Boy Scout, I'm still a virgin!"

Tosca walked over to the woman, taking her into his arms. "How nice of you to save yourself for me." He kissed her, then gave her a playful swat across the seat of her pants. "Now, let's go."

Rather than the Harley, Tosca and Jeri climbed into his '73 Ford Econoline, a weather-beaten van with tinted windows. Tosca could easily afford a better set of wheels, but he had a sentimental attachment to the vehicle and had replaced its engine twice over the years to keep it roadworthy.

Tosca made his way south from Ridon on Interstate 75, getting off at the exit to Eight Mile Road, which straddled the Macomb County line. He dropped off Jeri at her apartment, a high-priced condo down the road from Hazel Park Raceway, where she made a decent living hustling big winners at the clubhouse bar.

Contrary to what he'd told Scotty Sear, Tosca didn't need to be in Wyandotte for the cocaine shipment until later that evening. With the Renegades out tending to his unfinished business, he figured he had a few hours to kill. No stranger to the racetrack himself, Tosca decided to drive up to Hazel Park and play the ponies for a while. A few of his drug clients were regulars at the track, and if he caught any of them on a winning streak, he could probably find buyers for some of the coke that wasn't already spoken for.

He hadn't traveled far, however, when another, more tempting opportunity presented itself.

Three blocks away, a scrawny teenage boy was standing on a street corner, puffing on a cigarette as he waved bouquets of day-old roses at passing motorists. He'd picked a lousy location, because there were no buildings or homes around and hardly any traffic.

Tosca pulled over to the curb and left his engine running. Opening his glove compartment, he pulled out a handkerchief and a glass jar filled with chloroform. After rolling down his window, he opened the jar and soaked the handkerchief, then put the jar away and stuck the drenched cloth under the front passenger's seat. The potent fumes still drifted up, and Tosca opened the passenger's window as well to get some cross ventilation.

Shifting into gear, the hardman headed down the street, keeping his eye on traffic. A couple more cars drove past the teenager, neither stopping. Once they were out of view and he couldn't see any other cars approaching, Tosca sped up. He passed the youth as well, then quickly put on his brakes and pulled over.

As expected, the youth tossed aside his cigarette and ran to catch up with the van.

"Howdy," Tosca said to the youth as he peered in the passenger's window. "Those roses fresh?"

"No, they're very well-mannered," the kid joked. He couldn't have been more than fourteen. His face was pale, splashed with an array of freckles and acne. When he smiled, he revealed a mouthful of braces. "Just kidding. Yeah, they're pretty fresh. Buck apiece."

"I'll take ten." Tosca peeled a ten-dollar bill from his wallet and held it out.

When the boy reached inside and grabbed the bill, Tosca abruptly leaned over, seized the collar of the youth's shirt and jerked him forward until he was halfway into the van.

"Hey!" the boy cried out, struggling against his captor's iron grip.

Tosca quickly reached under the front seat for the handkerchief and clamped it over his victim's face, smothering his cries. The boy put up a fight for a few seconds longer, then suddenly went limp.

Tosca pulled him the rest of the way in, then shoved him into the back of the van. He checked the windows and rearview mirror, making sure that no other motorists had arrived on the scene. Satisfied the coast was clear, he put the van back into gear and drove off.

5

"I know this wasn't an easy decision for you," Bolan told George Simmons.

Helena's father eyed Bolan gravely. "I just hope you're right about all this. You have no idea what a toll this is taking on my wife."

The two men were standing in the front doorway of George and Toni Simmonses' small country home, located six miles down the road from the farm where Joey Simmonses' family had been gunned down. In the background, Helena was comforting her mother, who was visibly distraught. Bolan eyed the women, then turned back to George.

"I know it's painful," the warrior said, "but as long as the real killer is still out there, it's going to make the healing process that much more difficult."

"Then find him, whoever he is," George pleaded. "Whatever it takes..."

"We will," Bolan promised. "You have my word."

The two men shook hands. Helena shared a final embrace with her mother, then joined Bolan in the hallway. George gave her a kiss, then held her at arm's length, his large callused hands resting on her shoulders. "You're all we have left now, Hellie," he told her. "I know you have a mind of your own and I've never been able to tell you what to do, but please, for your mother's sake...stay out of this from here on in. Leave it to Mr. Belasko and the authorities."

"Dad, I'll be careful, okay?"

"That's not the answer I'm looking for."

"Don't ask me to lie to you, then," Helena said. She lowered her voice so her mother couldn't hear her. "I'm not going to just wring my hands and grieve if there's a way I can help to see that justice is done. I know what I have to do and I promise I'll be careful."

George stared at his daughter, then slowly took his hands away and stepped back. Offering a sad smile, he told her, "You got your stubbornness from me, so I can't very well fault you, now, can I?"

Helena stepped forward and kissed him. "I love you, Dad."

"And I love you."

"THAT WASN'T EASY," Helena said with a sigh as Bolan started the car and pulled out of the driveway.

"I know, but it was the right thing to do. Once the court order comes through and they exhume the bodies, we can hopefully find a fresh angle on looking for the killer."

"I sure hope so."

Once they were out on the open country road, they both fell silent. Bolan mulled over his conversation with Helena's father and his vow to track down the killer. For a man who never went back on his word, he'd just made quite a commitment, especially when one considered that the murders were, at best, only peripherally linked to the assignment that had brought Bolan to Michigan from Stony Man Farm.

Then why had he made such a promise? An obvious answer would have been the attractive woman sitting beside him, and Bolan couldn't deny that, on a certain level, he felt himself drawn to Helena. But it took more than a pretty face to sway the Executioner. He was, after all, a professional and knew better than to risk compromising his judgment by succumbing to personal motivations.

And yet, ultimately, it was just such a personal factor that did, in fact, lay at the root of Bolan's commitment to find the killer of Joey Simmons and his family, and he realized it for perhaps the first time as he was guiding the Mustang down that remote stretch of Michigan road.

The key lay in Bolan's past, half a lifetime ago, when he'd been plucked from his second tour of duty in the combat hell zone of Southeast Asia. All the while he'd been battling Charlie, Death ever at his door, Bolan had never considered that his family back in the States would ever find their own lives in danger. Yet when he'd returned to America, it had been to bury most of his loved ones.

It had been those murders that had propelled Mack Bolan into his present occupation. When he'd learned

that the obliteration of his family had been Mob related, Bolan had sworn vengeance and dedicated his
life to a one-man war against organized crime. For
years he'd wreaked havoc on the Families, not only in
his hometown but from coast to coast. It had been a
bloody campaign, a campaign that over the years had
expanded to include a more diverse but equally vi-
cious pool of enemies. Terrorists, foreign despots,
rogue intelligence agents, KGB...evil came in many
guises, and Bolan vowed that he wouldn't rest so long
as such elements still thrived off the pain and suffer-
ing of the innocent.

At the onset he'd operated solely on his own, without ties to any government, but in recent years he'd
become linked to Stony Man Farm, the outfit he'd
helped found and nurture into a vehicle of support
that could focus greater resources and manpower toward missions that, in this modern-day world, became increasingly difficult to be handled by one man
alone.

So, while Bolan was now part of a larger whole, he
still remained his own man, bound by his own code,
ever mindful of that first great loss that had made him
what he was today. When faced with circumstances
that so closely mirrored those of his own experience,
there was no way he could turn his back and let the
situation go unresolved.

"We'll find them," Bolan told Helena, breaking
their silence after they'd been driving for several miles.
Even as he was speaking, though, the warrior was be-

ginning to think that perhaps it was the killer, or killers, who had found him.

Within a block after leaving Helena's parents, Bolan had noticed a pair of motorcyclists pulling out from a side street and following the Mustang. Now, miles later and despite several turns onto different roads, the bikers were still visible in the rearview mirror, slowly gaining ground. With only rolling farmland on either side of the two-lane road, Bolan knew that if the bikers were planning to do more than just tail the Mustang, this was when they were going to make their move.

"Helena," Bolan said as he unzipped his coat, exposing the Beretta holstered in his shoulder harness, "I want you to be ready to lean forward when I tell you to, all right?"

To Bolan's surprise, Helena replied, "then you've noticed them, too."

"Yeah," the warrior stated, pressing his foot on the accelerator. The Mustang picked up speed, racing past a field lined with rows of dry, withered cornstalks.

NOT SURPRISINGLY the two motorcycles surged forward, as well. Brewster was astride one of the Harleys, the Renegades' emblem painted on the gas tank and sewn onto the back of his denim vest. Riding alongside him was Ronnie "Trickshot" Guinness, a twenty-year-old hardcase who'd been in and out of juvenile hall and jail for the past six years on a string of offenses ranging from shoplifting and vagrancy to aggravated assault and armed robbery. He was hoping to add murder to his résumé today, thereby ensuring his admittance into the Renegades.

Keeping his right hand on the throttle, Guinness reached inside his coat and pulled out a .38-caliber handgun. He'd learned a long time ago that shooting while "in the saddle" was nowhere near as easy as they made it look in the movies, but countless hours of practice had turned him into something of a legend among friends, who'd tagged him with the nickname Trickshot. When he took aim over his handlebars and squeezed the trigger, it took him only two shots to achieve his objective—taking out one of the front tires of the Mustang.

Almost immediately the car began to swerve out of control. Guinness beamed at his handiwork and slipped his gun back inside his coat. He shot a sideways glance at Brewster, who had armed himself with a sawed-off shotgun.

"Good shot!" Brewster shouted above the rumble of their engines. "Now let's go finish them off!"

BOLAN HAD JUST CLOSED his fingers around his Beretta when he'd spotted one of the bikers reaching for his gun. Quickly placing both hands on the steering wheel, the warrior shouted, "Down! Now!"

From inside the car, the first shot sounded like a muffled pop, especially in comparison to the louder sound of a bullet dinging off the right front quarter panel.

Helena leaned forward, reaching for her purse. Bolan didn't dare shift his gaze from the rearview mirror and the open road before him, but out of the corner of his eye he saw the woman reach into her purse and withdraw a palm-size .22 automatic.

"What do you think you're doing?" Bolan asked.

"Just what it looks like," Helena countered, releasing the gun's safety.

At that moment a second shot exploded the front tire. The Mustang lurched to one side, and Bolan fought the wheel, trying to right his course. But it was nearly impossible to thwart the speeding vehicle's momentum, and the Executioner knew better than to risk flipping the car by slamming on the brakes. As the Mustang began to go into a tailspin, the warrior shouted, "Stay loose and roll with it...we're going to crash!"

6

The Mustang spun wildly off the road, shearing a mileage marker and bounding over a shallow ditch into the wire fence surrounding the cornfield. Half-rotted wood posts were severed by the impact, and the fence itself flattened under the car's weight as it plowed through the cornstalks. The ground was still wet from recent rains, helping to slow the vehicle, but it still traveled well into the stalks before finally coming to a stop.

Brewster and Guinness pulled off the road and stopped near the break in the fence, idling their choppers as they peered into the field.

"Can't see them."

"Easy enough to follow their tracks," Brewster replied over the throaty drone of his engine. "Let's ditch our bikes in the corn and finish them off on foot."

Guinness nodded, coaxing his Harley slowly over the downed wire and into the first row of corn. Once he felt sure he was beyond sight from the road, he killed the engine and set the bike down on a a bed of toppled stalks. Brewster did the same, turning the field suddenly and strangely silent.

"Let's split up," Brewster whispered, indicating he'd circle around from his right. Sawed-off shotgun held in one huge fist, he headed off into the corn.

Guinness hung back a moment, reloading his gun. He still felt euphoric over the way he'd blown out the Mustang's tire with only his second shot. Brewster had to be impressed, he thought. Now all he had to do was wrap up the job and he, too, would finally be able to wear the Renegade colors. Yeah, it was going to be great. As part of the gang, he'd be in on all kinds of action, be able to have his pick from all kinds of hot broads who were always looking to get laid by bikers. Hell, once he was through the initiation, he bet they'd let him celebrate by being in on one of those gang bangs he'd heard so much about. There was even a chance the woman they'd been tracking would still be alive, in which case she'd do nicely.

But first he had to track her down and make sure the guy with her was dead. Brewster had said it would be best if it looked like the crash killed him, but Guinness secretly hoped it wouldn't be that easy. Sure, he'd get credit for murdering the guy, but it seemed like such a pansy way to pass his initiation. He was interested more in something like an Old West showdown, where he could face down his foe before showing him why he was called Trickshot.

As Guinness started into the cornfield, a sudden breeze picked up, stirring the dry stalks around him. It was an unsettling noise, and the biker stopped in his tracks, swinging around to take aim at a sound just off to his left. He held back on pulling the trigger at the last second, when he realized it was only the wind shaking the limbs of an old weather-beaten scarecrow that had half fallen from its perch. Straw spilled like gold shafts of blood from the figure's unbuttoned shirt.

Guinness stepped wide of the scarecrow as he began stalking the lost Mustang. The wind continued to blow, rustling more stalks and further unnerving the biker. Crows startled from the field had taken refuge on a power line. When one of them squawked, the eerie caw sounded like taunting laughter.

"Shut up!" Guinness hissed as he glared at the birds. They ignored him, however, and another of the creatures cackled as it shifted its position on the wire, gently flapping its wings. It was a foreboding sight, particularly to Guinness, who, as a child, had sat through several viewings of Alfred Hitchcock's *The Birds*. A part of him felt that at any moment the crows were going to fly down in unison and begin pecking at him with their beaks.

Get a grip, he ordered himself as he inched through the corn. He was glad Brewster had split off. If anybody saw him now, half-spooked by a little wind and some loudmouthed birds, he'd never live it down.

As Brewster suggested, it was easy enough to see which way the Mustang had gone. The beaten path through the corn was wide enough that Guinness could keep it in sight while he remained a few rows back, using untouched stalks for cover.

Finally he saw the car. From his angle of approach, it was difficult to see any sign of movement inside the vehicle. He looked past the Mustang, trying to spot Brewster converging from the other direction. But there was no sign of him.

"Well, here goes..." Guinness murmured, raising his gun into firing position. A downed cornstalk snapped under his weight as he made his way forward.

A sudden blur of activity flashed to the biker's right. Before he could react, Bolan burst through the amber curtain. His first move was to level a full-force karate chop at Guinness's wrist, knocking the gun from his hand without it going off. Then, as a follow-up to the same motion, the Executioner whipped his elbow up at a sharp angle, clipping the young thug's throat with so much force that he could hear the windpipe snap. Any attempt to cry out was strangled as Guinness staggered backward, choking. Totally overwhelmed by the surprise attack, he put up little further resistance as Bolan dragged him to the ground and took him permanently out of play.

The warrior had hoped to dispatch the attacker without alerting his buddy, but apparently he'd failed, because as he was rising to his knees, he heard a stunned gasp that he instantly knew was Helena finding herself confronted back near the Mustang.

Bolan raced forward, trying to reach the car in time, but he was still a few yards away when a shotgun blast roared through the corn.

The warrior scrambled around the vehicle, bracing himself for the worst. To his amazement, however, he found Brewster sprawled out dead on the ground, his shotgun lying beside him. Helena was still sitting in the front seat of the Mustang, with the buckshot-riddled door hanging half-open. She was still holding her .22 in firing position, aiming it at the dead man on the ground. Her face was ashen, filled with a horrible realization.

"He was going to kill me," she whispered numbly as Bolan approached her. "He was going to kill me...."

He'd nearly succeeded, too. Glancing down, Bolan saw blood seeping through Helena's coat. The woman continued to stare at Brewster, oblivious to her wound, already in a state of shock. Bolan slowly reached out and took the gun from her hand.

"It's all right," he told her.

"He was going to kill me," she whispered again.

A LITTLE LESS than twenty miles away, Rosey Tosca drove his van across an old brick bridge that offered a view of Lake Jeltz, one of the larger bodies of water in Macomb County. A few boats were out, most of them anchored near clusters of lily pads on the far shore, where the best fishing was. Two fishermen stood against the bridge's railing, staring down at where their lines dipped into the cold autumn waters, waiting for something to bite.

"Hey, guys, I already caught mine." Tosca chuckled as he drove past. "And he's a keeper."

The teenager he'd apprehended earlier was sprawled out in the back of the van, blindfolded, gagged, and bound at the wrist and ankles. He was just starting to regain consciousness. When Tosca took a corner sharply, the youth slid across the floor and slammed into the side of the van, crushing his roses. He let out a garbled moan.

"Almost there, amigo," Tosca called out to him.

After passing a summer youth camp that was closed for the season, Tosca slowed and turned onto a private side road. A six-foot-high wall made of mortar and river rock surrounded a sprawling twenty-acre lakeside estate. Forty yards off the main road a security booth stood outside a gated entryway. The sign posted over the gate identified the establishment as The Beta Institute.

Tosca slowed to a stop alongside the security booth. He rolled down his tinted window and grinned at the uniformed security agent.

"Howdy, Dennis."

"Good afternoon, sir," said the guard, a man in his early twenties with crew-cut hair and the no-nonsense look of a well-trained private fresh out of boot camp. He pressed a button on the console in front of him, and the wrought-iron gates slowly began to open.

"As you were," Tosca told the guard, snapping off a mock salute as he put the van back in gear and drove through the gate.

At first there was nothing to see but endless rows of evenly spaced, well-established pine trees that flanked the road and shrouded it in deep shadows.

Then the trees abruptly gave way to a small, open campus. There were fourteen buildings of various sizes, none of them older than a few years, all of them similar in design and built low to blend in with the surrounding landscape. At first glance one might have surmised they were looking at a quaint little private university, probably focused on the liberal arts and attended by well-heeled, spoiled children of automobile executives and other members of the upper crust. Such a misconception was the intent of the institute's founder. In fact the campus *had* been modeled after an elite private college in Los Angeles.

A few people were on the grounds, but nothing compared to the bustle of a university in midsemester. It wasn't until Tosca had rounded a bend and come upon a large outdoor amphitheater that he spotted a cluster of twenty young men and women attending what could have passed for an outdoor lecture. Through his open window, however, he could tell that something besides class was in session.

In unison the "students" gathered in the amphitheater began to chant. Tosca thought it might be Latin, or possibly Spanish. Rolling up his window to shut out the sound, he tapped his fingers on the steering wheel and whistled along with the song playing on the radio.

He might have appeared bored, but the truth of the matter was that despite three years of association with the Beta Institute, Tosca still felt uneasy whenever he passed through the front gates. There was something about the whole enterprise that tapped into a dark, elemental part of his psyche. His feelings of fascination and fear took him back to his childhood, when he'd have vivid nightmares after watching late-night horror movies on television. Of course, the obvious solution back then would have been to just avoid such movies, but Tosca found he couldn't. He found himself drawn to the sensation he felt after waking from the nightmares—the quickened pulse, the heightened state of alertness, the feeling that he'd been drawn into a different and somehow more vital world. Over the years he'd found he could approximate some of those same sensations by ingesting drugs or committing crimes, but his dealings with Beta came even closer to invoking that wondrous state. Here, behind the tranquil facades and beautiful surroundings, was a surreal land of mad scientists and living zombies, of Frankensteins and Mr. Hydes. For Tosca, dealing with such a world without being sucked into it was an incomparable high. To be paid exorbitantly for his participation made the game that much more thrilling.

Tosca drove past the amphitheater and several adjacent buildings, then pulled into a driveway leading past a sign that read Office of the Dean. The driveway wound up through another belt of thick pines, bringing him to a two-story building built into the side of a 112-foot-high man-made mountain. The garage and parking facilities were both located atop the mountain. Tosca pulled into a parking space near the main entrance, stopped his engine and climbed out of the van.

A tall man wearing a uniform similar to the security guard at the main gate emerged from the garage. Strapped to his thigh was a holster containing an Uzi machine pistol.

"I need a wheelchair," Tosca told him as he circled around the van.

"I'll get one," the other man replied, promptly heading back into the garage. He emerged moments later rolling a wheelchair before him. Once Tosca opened the back of his van, he motioned for the guard to help him drag the teenage boy out. The youth tried to resist, squirming and kicking as best he could with his feet bound together.

"Hey, knock it off!" Tosca snapped, cuffing the youth on the back of the head, then pinning him down while the guard unclipped something from the shirt pocket of his uniform. It looked like a pen, but when he pulled off the cap, a hypodermic needle gleamed in the afternoon light. The guard rammed the needle into the teenager's shoulder.

The youth tensed as the needle sank in, then began to weep as the guard extracted it and tossed it into a nearby trash receptacle. Putting up no further resistance, the boy was transferred into the wheelchair, then strapped in place with a series of leather belts.

"I can take it from here," Tosca said, stepping behind the wheelchair. "Just get the door for me."

The guard complied, and Tosca wheeled his captive into what was essentially a rooftop greenhouse. Rows of flowering plants lined the glass walls of the structure, filling the air with their combined fragrance. Two men in lab coats were huddled over one cluster of plants, carefully taking pollen samples and making notations on clipboards. Behind them was a panoramic view of Lake Jeltz and the back acreage of the institute, which was composed primarily of more pine groves and a few small garden areas.

The men briefly regarded Tosca and the blindfolded youth in the wheelchair, then silently returned to their work. Tosca wheeled his charge across the greenhouse to an elevator. As he waited for the doors to open, he told the youth, "Too bad you couldn't get a job selling *these* flowers. Lot of them are as rare as hell, especially in this part of the world."

The youth didn't respond, however. The injection had knocked him out and he slumped awkwardly to one side in the wheelchair, his jaw hanging slack.

When the elevator doors opened, Tosca wheeled the youth in, then pressed for the ground floor.

"You're gonna like this place," the hardman said. "Just wait and see."

The elevator slowed to a stop and the doors opened again. Tosca pushed the wheelchair out into a windowless, brightly illuminated corridor. At the first corner, he turned to his right and started down an even longer passageway. He didn't get far, however, before a door swung open and a familiar figure stepped out, blocking the way.

"What the fuck are you doing here?" Frankie Cerdae demanded. "You're supposed to be taking out that Simmons woman.

"It's being taken care of."

"You were supposed to take care of it yourself."

"I don't remember anybody saying that," Tosca retorted. "Besides, I was busy with this guy."

Cerdae reined in his temper as he looked the youth over. "Runaway?"

Tosca shook his head. "Flower vendor."

"Same difference."

"He's a real fighter when he's awake," Tosca promised. "Perfect subject."

"Well, we'll see what the boss says," Cerdae said, moving in to take control of the wheelchair. He eyed Tosca with disdain. "I suppose you want the usual."

"You bet," the hardman replied, hitching his belt. "And, hey, don't knock it till you try it."

"I think I'll pass." Cerdae gestured toward one of the doors halfway down the hall. "I think there's one in there. Help yourself."

"Don't mind if I do, Frankie. Don't mind if I do...."

As Cerdae wheeled the teenager away, Tosca ventured to the door and swung it open. Taking a step inside, he beamed with expectation. The room was small and dimly lighted. There was no furniture except for a single bed, upon which lay a teenage girl in a hospital smock that barely covered her blooming flesh. She was breathing shallowly but gave no sign of having heard Tosca enter the room.

"Hey, you're a real beaut, sweetheart."

Tosca closed the door behind him and locked it. He moved to the bed and leaned over the girl, raising her right hand and then letting it fall limply back onto the bed. If she was like most of the others, she'd be heavily sedated for at least another couple hours. Plenty of time for him to have some fun.

7

"She's lost a lot of blood and the buckshot cracked a few ribs, but there's no serious damage," the doctor reported. "She'll need time to recuperate, though."

"Thanks, Doc," Bolan said.

The doctor excused himself, leaving Bolan alone with Hal Brognola, Stony Man Farm's chief of operations. They were at the infirmary on Mosenan Isle, a small island on the Detroit River near Wyandotte. Owned by the U.S. military, Mosenan housed a three-acre high-security facility devoted almost exclusively to biochemical research. Gerley Chemical was their primary supplier of lab materials, as well as an ongoing subcontractor on a variety of classified research projects. The connection was a matter of concern for Bolan. Brognola sensed it and tried to offer some assurance.

"Don't worry, Striker. We'll keep her under round-the-clock protection. She'll be fine."

"I'm not so sure." Bolan quickly told Brognola about the investigative piece she'd written for *Detroit Monthly* on Gerley Chemical, concluding, "She's nearly been killed twice in the past two days. It might be just a coincidence, but what if someone wants her silenced because they're afraid she's sitting on some valuable information, something that could crack the case for us?''

"That seems farfetched," Brognola said. "Remember, she wasn't necessarily a target in either incident. She happened to be in the wrong place at the wrong time at Bridony's trailer, and today I suspect you were the one the bikers were after.''

"We don't know that for sure," Bolan persisted. "What if I'm right? If there's a security breach at Gerley's plant in Talville, who's to say there aren't turncoats here on the island, too?''

Brognola had arrived in Michigan three hours earlier, having been summoned from the Farm in the aftermath of Don White's murder. Two of those hours had been spent in a briefing with top-level officials looking into the security problems at Gerley. The level of frustration had been high, with everyone expressing concern at the lack of progress in flushing out the forces responsible for smuggling biochemical materials and classified information out of the Talville plant. When word had been received on the attempted murder of Bolan and Helena Simmons, a plan of action had been formulated. Brognola had vehemently opposed the strategy, but he was overruled and left with the miserable task of breaking the news to Bolan.

"She'll be safe here," the big Fed repeated. "We're bringing in outside security. Nobody with any link to Gerley.''

"Maybe not right here." Bolan walked to a window and pointed to the buildings on the other side of the island. "But what about over there? There're people there who deal with Gerley all the time. If they catch wind that Helena's holed up here, they might..."

Bolan's voice trailed off, and he stared at his friend with narrowed eyes.

Brognola nodded gravely. "Yes, they might try to do something about it. And if they do, we'll be watching. We have her apartment back in Talville under surveillance, too. If someone shows up there, we'll be on top of them."

"So she's bait."

"It wasn't my decision, Striker. I don't happen to agree with it, either, but you know what the stakes are. Sometimes you have to take drastic measures."

They were interrupted when an Army officer entered the room, handing a cablegram to Brognola.

"Thank you." As the officer left, the big Fed opened the envelope and glanced at the last line on the message. "It's from the Farm," he told Bolan. "Give me a second to read this over."

A moment later Brognola glanced up. "Able Team's just wrapped up their assignment in San Diego. I can bring them in here to handle security. How about it?"

Able Team was a three-man hell squad of Stony Man Farm's finest warriors, routinely assigned to domestic missions similar to those Bolan contended with. The Executioner had fought side by side with them on countless occasions and found them to be the cream of the crop. Aside from a few other members of the Stony Man elite, he could think of no one he'd trust more to see a mission through.

"Damn straight."

"Then it's a done deal."

Brognola then turned his attention to a thin pile of notes spread out on the table before him. "As far as who's been making drops outside Gerley's parking lot, we've ruled out two of the three shifts. But that still leaves us with nearly two dozen suspects with hands-on access to the stuff that's been smuggled out. If you figure it might also be somebody who's bypassing security, that's another seventy people to check out. And, of course, we're still considering the chance that the mole's working out of security. In short, it's going to take some time."

"Well, when the bad guys get those papers from the drop and realize they're bogus, they're going to know we're closing in on them," Bolan said. "Maybe somebody in the chain will panic and tip themselves off."

"Exactly."

The Executioner sipped his coffee, trying to figure out what other angles needed consideration. "What about Don White's killer? Any leads?"

"They ran ballistics on the bullets they pulled out of him—.22-caliber popgun. Not apt to be much help."

"Maybe we'll have better luck with that biker's shotgun," Bolan suggested. "If we can get a match with the wounds on the Simmons family, it could be a major breakthrough.''

"But we already know that the murder weapon was found in Ken Bridony's house trailer," Brognola reminded Bolan.

"One of the murder weapons. Without thorough autopsies, who's to say there wasn't a second shotgun?''

"Good point," Brognola conceded. "it's definitely worth looking into. And as for this Renegade biker gang, I'm expecting a full report by midafternoon, but preliminaries seem to show they've got their hands in all kinds of illicit action. Drugs, prostitution, armed robbery, a handful of killings . . .''

"And attempted killings," Bolan added.

"Right."

The Executioner glanced at his watch. "They're going to be exhuming the Simmons family in a couple hours. I want to be there. Is there anything else you need me for here?''

"Let me see . . .''

As Brognola was sifting through his notes, the door to the waiting room opened again and in walked Jack Grimaldi. He and the Executioner had been allied since Bolan's initial war with the Mob, and over the years they'd fought together more times than either could remember. Grimaldi's specialty was aviation, but he'd been pressed into other duties as part of Stony Man operations and proved himself to be as valuable outside the cockpit as he was inside.

"Heard you had another close call today," he told Bolan as he sprawled into a vacant chair and handed a manila folder to Brognola.

"Just my usual ration."

"What do we have here?" Brognola asked as he opened the file.

"Background check on Ken Bridony," the pilot reported. "He fits the profile. Loner, paranoid, brilliant at a few things, Bone dumb at a lot more. He'd been living at the trailer park for a little over four months."

"Any link with Gerley Chemical?" Bolan asked.

"Other than living on the other side of the woods from them, no," Grimaldi said. "I mean, he had a few prescriptions that were Gerley drugs, but the odds are half the people in Michigan do, too."

Brognola raised an eyebrow as he skimmed one of the computer readouts. "According to this, Bridony didn't have a registration for a shotgun."

"Yeah," Grimaldi speculated, "but he could have stolen it, bought it on the black market...got it any number of ways."

"I still say it had to be planted by whoever killed him and Don White," Bolan maintained. "And it wasn't a teenage runaway."

Bolan flipped through the readout and found something else that intrigued him. "What's this about his being a student? I thought he was in his thirties."

"Thirty-two. He was just taking a class in computer programming," Grimaldi said, pointing at the readout. "This Beta Institute's some kind of glorified self-help academy. They run occupational programs for the public, but they have a lot of live-ins, too."

"Dormitories?" Brognola asked.

"Not exactly," Grimaldi replied. "Near as I can figure the campus is split in two. Besides the occupational classes, there's a separate therapy facility. You know, part detox center, part one of those places where folks send their teenagers when they get out of hand. It's privately owned and operated. They keep a low profile, and there's no record of them running afoul of the law."

"I wonder..." Brognola speculated. "Maybe there's a connection between these problem kids and Bridony being a suspect in those kidnappings of teenagers."

"How?" Bolan wondered.

"I don't know. Maybe he just went to this school as an excuse to be around young kids. We haven't determined if he had some kind of fetish or anything, but if he did, it sounds like the ideal place for him to prowl."

"And not just that," Grimaldi said. "If there's any validity to this theory Bridony was killed by his accomplice in the Simmons murders, maybe that's where he partnered up."

"The guy I tangled with in the forest wasn't a teenager."

"And neither was Bridony," Grimaldi reminded Bolan. "If he was enrolled in one of the occupational classes, there were probably other adults, too."

"It's worth looking into," Brognola said.

"I'll get right on it," the Stony Man pilot said. "I want to check on some of his other work contacts and sniff around the trailer park a little more, too. Something's bound to turn up."

ROSEY TOSCA LAY IN BED, the unconscious young woman sprawled across him. They were both naked. Tosca had been in the room more than an hour, satisfying his various needs, and now, spent and reflective, he stared up at the overhead light built into the ceiling.

By now, he figured, the Simmons woman and the guy who'd saved her were probably history, and Scotty Sear was probably on his way to make sure there wouldn't by any incriminating autopsies of the slain family. Two major headaches were out of the way, and still a few hours remained before he had to be in Wyandotte. A stop at the athletic club was definitely in order, he decided. He'd soak in the whirlpool, bask in the sauna, arrange to have that fat Swede give him a long massage, then get dressed and treat himself to filet mignon and a good bottle of vintage wine at McWitt's on Olympic Avenue. After all that, he'd feel on top of the world, a man in charge and ready to deal with the Bolivians.

Tosca's daydreaming was cut short by a series of loud raps on the door.

"Boss wants to see you," Cerdae called through the door. "Get dressed and haul your ass outta there!"

"Say please," Tosca taunted.

"Fuck off!"

Tosca heard Cerdae retreat from the door. He slowly pushed the young woman off him, then sat up in bed, reaching for his clothes. As he dressed, he stared at his latest victim. If she was like the others, she'd wake up with no inkling of what had happened to her. The "counselors" would tell her whatever they felt would best serve their objective of breaking down her free will and turning her into a worker who could be counted on to be devoutly loyal and grateful for her lowly position at the institute.

Once he was dressed, Tosca left the room and started down the hallway. Reaching a tall archway, he stepped into a huge antechamber, almost blinding in its whiteness. Cerdae was nowhere to be seen. The only other person in the chamber was the man responsible for the creation of the Beta Institute as well as all of its ongoing projects; the man Frankie Cerdae was assigned to protect.

The boss was Dr. Mark Dykes, a pallid, stoop-shouldered man in his early sixties. His Vandyke beard was the same silverish hue as his neatly cropped hair, and he had clear blue eyes behind his wire-rimmed glasses. Glancing up from his clipboard, he offered Tosca a warm smile and extended a large, bony hand.

"Rosey, my lad," he called out jovially, shaking Tosca's hand. "You brought us a good one this time. Strictly first-rate."

"Glad to hear it."

"I thought you might like to see what we've done with him."

"Sure, why not?" Tosca said with a shrug.

"Why not indeed!" Dykes clapped his hands and motioned for Tosca to follow him as he started across the room. "Come on, he's right over here...."

They approached one of several large windows in the room. When Dykes pressed a switch mounted next to the window frame, a thin retractable shade rolled up into the wall, revealing that the window was in fact a two-way mirror allowing the men to look into the adjacent room without being seen by those inside. There were two people in the room, sitting in chairs on either side of a table. One was a woman in her early forties, wearing a plain blue dress, the other the youth Tosca had brought in.

"He's been a perfect subject," Dykes told Tosca as they observed. "Stubborn and totally uncooperative. We suspect he's a runaway as well as a vendor, but he won't say where he's from, who his parents are, why he ran away... nothing."

"But that's about to change, right?"

"Precisely." Dykes glanced at his watch. "We gave him the serum just a few minutes ago. Let's cross our fingers, shall we?"

As Tosca stared through the window, Dykes toggled a switch allowing them to hear what was taking place in the other room.

"What's your name?" the woman asked.

"Jim," the boy responded offhandedly.

"Jim what?"

"Jim Claney."

The youth drummed his fingers on the tabletop, bobbing his head. His eyes were clear, and he showed no signs of being drugged. There were also no signs of his earlier resistance or any apparent awareness of the circumstances by which he'd been brought here. To look at him, one might have guessed he was nothing more than a curious high-school student dropping in on a counselor to get some advice about how to fill out college applications.

"And where are you from, Jim Claney?" the woman asked.

Without hesitation, the boy replied, "California. Anaheim." With an impish smile, he added, "Couple blocks from the ballpark. You know, the Angels?"

"Yes. And do your parents still live in Anaheim?"

"Sure do," the boy said. "My dad's a cop and my mom, she's a housewife."

"I see," the woman said. "And why did you leave home?"

"Got tired of Dad beating me up."

As the interrogation continued, Dykes turned to his companion, beaming. "Not bad, hmm?"

Tosca was impressed. "You're saying that before he had the serum he wouldn't tell you any of this?"

"Not a word," Dykes said with a laugh. "As a matter of fact, up until five minutes ago, we weren't sure if there were any more words in his vocabulary than, 'Fuck off.'"

"Well, he sure doesn't seem to have any qualms about talking now," Tosca observed.

"That's right. And, if all works out as I expect, once the drug wears off, he'll fall asleep, then wake up with no recollection that any of this happened."

"So it's kind of like hypnosis," Tosca guessed.

"In a way," Dykes admitted. "Only it's taken me more than twenty years to get to this point."

"No kidding," Tosca said as he watched the youth casually light a cigarette inside the other room. "And those papers I brought to your place last night . . . did they help any?"

Dykes smiled. "We need to talk about that, Rosey. But that can be later."

The hardman frowned, suddenly on his guard. "What's the matter? I brought you everything."

"I'm sure you did. But, please, let's not worry about that right now. This is more import—wait a second! What's this?"

Inside the other room, something had suddenly gone wrong. One minute the youth was laughing as he talked with the woman and puffed away on his cigarette, the next he was on his feet, gasping for breath and clawing at his throat. The woman stood and circled the table to help him.

Dykes reached for an intercom next to the door and keyed the microphone, shouting, "Code Blue, room 5! Code Blue, room 5!"

Tosca followed Dykes into the room, where the teenager had slumped to the floor. His face had turned blue. The woman tilted his head back and started CPR. Moments later, Frankie Cerdae charged into the room along with two men in lab coats who were carrying syringes and a portable defibrillator. Tosca stood back as the others huddled over the fallen youth, attempting in various ways to revive him. When mouth-to-mouth failed and several injections produced no results, the defibrillators were placed on his bared chest and an electrical charge was passed through them. The body jerked wildly, but the youth's heart failed to resume beating.

"We lost him," Dykes finally conceded, all traces of his earlier euphoria gone from his face. "I don't believe it."

"It happened right after he started smoking the cigarette," the woman observed.

"I know that!"

"But right up until then it was going great," Tosca told him. "So you must be pretty close, right?"

"How should I know?" Dykes shouted. "Maybe there's a connection with the cigarette, or maybe it was a coincidence, right? I'll have to cut him up to find out." The doctor snatched up the youth's cigarette pack and hurled it at the wall, then stormed out of the room.

"Okay, okay," Cerdae said, stepping in to restore order. He reached under the dead youth's shoulders and gestured for one of the medics to grab his legs. "Let's get him out of here."

Tosca watched the body being carried away, then turned to the woman, who was clearly upset by the ordeal.

"How many times has that happened?" he asked.

The woman drew in a deep breath and said, "Nothing happened."

"What are you talking about?" Tosca said.

"Do you understand me?" the woman insisted. "Nothing happened . . ."

8

Sheriff Hough was waiting outside his patrol car when Bolan arrived at Farthing Meadows Cemetery.

"Rented another Mustang, eh?" Hough said as Bolan got out of his car. "Must not be the superstitious type, I guess."

"I guess not."

The tension between the two men was obvious, but neither was about to offer the first apology.

"Paperwork's all taken care of," Hough said, patting a bulge in the breast pocket of his coat. "Coroner's already at the grave sites. They wanted to get started while they still have plenty of daylight."

"Fine by me," Bolan replied.

They started up a gentle slope, following a flagstone walkway. The grounds were rolling and strewed not only with gravestones but also brightly colored leaves shed by tall Dutch elms that stood in stark relief against the overcast sky. As they passed a row of overgrown shrubs, Bolan noticed the crumbling remains of an old brick wall poking up through the leaves.

"A building?" Bolan queried.

"Sanatorium," Hough told him, gesturing around. "Years back, all this used to be an insane asylum. After it shut down, nobody could get up the nerve to develop the land and we got tired of transients camping out and starting the buildings on fire, so we blew them all up. Instant cemetery. And the dead don't mind much that this used to be a nuthouse, you know?"

"I suppose they don't."

"You know, on the way over here, I gave George and Toni Simmons a call," Hough told Bolan. "They're a mite spooked about having armed guards posted outside their house."

"Can't blame them, can you?" Bolan asked.

"No, sir, I can't," the sheriff confessed. "I mentioned to them that their daughter's being protected, too. They asked me where. Of course, I couldn't tell them, seeing how I don't know...."

"And I'm not at liberty to tell you. But she's in good hands."

"Yeah, well, George tells me you said the same thing to him," Hough drawled, "and the next thing he knew Helena nearly got herself blown to kingdom come."

Bolan wasn't interested in being dawn into an argument. He looked away from the sheriff. Up ahead, a groundskeeper sat at the controls of a small power shovel, scooping up the earth in front of a gravestone with the name Joseph James Simmons chiseled on its polished facing. The coroner stood nearby, his face

expressionless as he watched. He wouldn't be conducting the autopsies until the bodies were taken back
to the county morgue, but he'd been asked to accom-
pany Hough and witness the proceedings as a contin-
gency of the court order mandating the exhumations.

"You know, Belasko," Hough persisted, "I can
handle the fact that you don't like me, because, among
other things, the feeling's mutual. But the feeling I'm
getting here is that you don't trust me, either, and that
bothers me."

"Sorry you feel that way, but it's nothing personal."

"Yeah, right."

Hough introduced Bolan to the coroner, then the
three men watched silently as the groundskeeper pulled
up more dirt and transferred it to a growing mound
several feet away. The warrior noticed the gravestones of Joey's wife and children. Fresh sod had been
laid over the graves only a couple weeks earlier, but
already it had blended in with the surrounding grass.
Clearly the graves hadn't been disturbed since the
burial services.

A few minutes later, the groundskeeper emptied a
final scoop with the power shovel, then turned off the
engine and scrambled down to the ground. He picked
up a spade and called over another worker who was
digging up weeds around a family plot twenty feet
away. Climbing down into the hole, the two men
carefully shoveled up small scoops of dirt until they
had unearthed Joey Simmons's casket. It took an-

other five minutes to secure straps to the coffin and run them up into the same power winch that had been used to lower Joey to what was supposed to have been his final resting place. While that was being done, Bolan and the sheriff prepared the wheeled cart that would be used to transfer the coffin to a five-ton truck parked fifty yards away.

"I feel like a goddamn grave robber," the sheriff muttered as he and Bolan rolled the cart to the edge of the hole.

Once the casket had been raised as high as it would go, the groundskeepers turned off the winch, then took up positions on either side of the box, taking hold of its handles. Bolan and Hough secured grips as well, and on a count of three, the four men hefted the coffin clear of the winch.

"Awfully damn light," Hough grumbled. "Hell, Joey weighed more than two hundred pounds."

Bolan bent into a half crouch and peered underneath the casket. To his surprise, he saw that most of the bottom had been ripped away, exposing the inside, which was clearly empty.

"The body's gone," Bolan told them.

ON HIS DAYS OFF, Todd Jeffler moonlighted as a driver for Sanicorp, Ltd., a Detroit-based company specializing in hazardous-waste disposal. Thanks to cutthroat underbidding, zealous entrepreneurship and shadow backing by the Bariggia crime syndicate, Sanicorp had pretty much cornered the Michigan market in recent years, counting among its clients one of the Big Three automakers, major pharmaceutical plants in Kalamazoo, Niles and Lansing, and four military installations in the lower peninsula.

And, of course, Sanicorp was also under contract with Gerley Chemical.

As he'd done every Tuesday afternoon for the past five months, Jeffler pulled up to the gate at Gerley at half-past two. Riding in the front seat next to him was Pedro Billings, a longtime member of the Renegades bike club, though it'd be hard to tell it from the looks of him. Like Jeffler, the biker was wearing a thick, bright yellow slicker over matching slacks, gloves and boots. Dangling around his neck was a specialized mask that, when pulled on in the event of emergency, could effectively counter the effects of any number of accidents involving the spillage or unexpected release of toxic materials.

A guard brought a clipboard over to the Sanicorp truck, handing it up to Jeffler once he'd opened his window.

"Hey, Floyd, how's it hanging?" Jeffler asked the guard as he scribbled his signature on a standardized security clearance form.

"Hanging just fine, Todd," the guard replied. He acknowledged Pedro with a perfunctory nod, then asked Jeffler, "You like the Pistons tonight?"

"Hell, yes," Jeffler said as he handed the clipboard back. "Twelve points."

"Ooh, sounds like I hear a bet." The guard handed a pair of visitor ID tags to Jeffler. "How's twenty bucks sound?"

"You're on."

Jeffler shifted the truck into gear as the guard stepped back and signaled another man to raise the swing arm blocking the entrance. Once the way was clear, Jeffler drove into the complex and circled around the first building he came to, backing up to a loading dock festooned with warning stickers proclaiming the presence of assorted hazardous wastes in the immediate vicinity.

Leaving the engine running, the two men exited the cab and climbed onto the loading dock. There was a buzzer on the wall next to the main door. Jeffler pressed it, then stepped back, waiting for a response. Pedro glanced around nervously.

"You sure it's a good idea for us to be doing this?" he asked, "especially with all the investigating that's going on?"

"What would you suggest we do, amigo? Start missing pickups? You think that won't rouse a lot more suspicion than carrying on as if nothing were wrong?"

Pedro mulled it over and shrugged. "I don't know, I guess maybe you're right."

"Of course I'm right. Maybe that's why I'm calling the shots."

"Oh, I thought maybe it was just because your brother's one of the guards here."

Jeffler shot Pedro a warning glance. "Nobody likes a wise guy. Understand?"

"Loud and clear. I hear you loud and clear."

"Good," Jeffler said.

A moment later the door opened, and the men were ushered into the main warehouse by Tim Jeffler, Todd's younger brother.

"Hey, bro," Todd said, giving Tim a good-natured punch on the shoulder. "You going to lay some waste on us?"

"Don't I always?" Tim nodded to the far side of the warehouse, where several fifty-gallon barrels were strapped securely onto the back of a wooden skid.

"Let's get cracking," Jeffler told Pedro. "I don't want to see my baby brother blow a gasket."

Pedro started across the room. Jeffler lingered a moment to be alone with his brother.

"We've got problems, Todd," Tim said. "Big problems..."

WHILE THE GROUNDSKEEPERS set Joey Simmons's empty coffin on the pallbearer's cart, Bolan and Hough moved back to the grave site and stared into the hole. They could see stray, splintered bits of the coffin mixed in with the loose dirt, as well as a smaller opening, the size of a manhole, just underneath where the casket had been laid to rest.

"I'll be damned," the sheriff muttered with disbelief.

Bolan quickly shook off his own incredulity and grabbed hold of one of the winch straps, using it to support his weight as he lowered himself into the cavity. Once he reached bottom, he let go of the strap and yanked out his Beretta. Peering into the smaller hole, he called out to Hough, "I can't see very far in, but it looks like it goes down at an angle."

When he saw Bolan lower his legs into the second hole, Hough gasped. "What are you doing?"

"I want to see where this leads to."

"Are you nuts? Who knows what the hell might be down there?"

"I'm going to find out."

As he squirmed down the hole, loose dirt tumbled in around him. As the Executioner had guessed, the shaft went down at close to a forty-five-degree angle, allowing him to move slowly, feeling his way with his feet. Once he was completely inside the narrow shaft, he paused a moment, waiting for his eyes to adjust to the change in light. The ground around him was cold and wet. He could hear himself breathing in the confined quarters, but there was no other sound except for that of more gravel tumbling into the opening.

Bolan had descended only another few yards when he came upon an offshoot tunnel, this one horizontal. He carefully reached inside the opening, gun at the ready. Unable to feel or to see anything, he decided to continue downward. He didn't go far before his feet suddenly lost touch with solid ground and dangled in an open space. He cautiously wriggled his way down farther, then swung his legs forward. They brushed up against something hard and flat. A wall. He moved one leg back and forth and finally came in contact with what felt like the rung of a ladder. Twisting his body, the warrior was able to pull himself the rest of the way out of the shaft and lower himself down the ladder until his feet were on solid ground. His movements echoed in both directions on either side of him, giving him some inkling of what he'd stumbled upon.

"There's some kind of tunnel down here," he shouted up to Hough. "Tiled walls, concrete floor."

By now Hough had lowered himself into the grave, and Bolan could see him silhouetted in the smaller opening. "It's got to be one of the tunnels from the asylum," he explained. "They had a whole network of them so they could move patients from building to building without letting them outside. Didn't want them running off."

"I'm going to see where this one goes."

"Well, you're on your own," Hough told him. "This is too weird. Invasion of the goddamn body snatchers, for Chrissakes!"

Bolan tuned out the sheriff and began groping his way down the tunnel. Each step drew him into a deeper, colder darkness. The smell of rot and decay was overpowering, but he was determined to forge on.

After more than thirty yards, the warrior came to a bend in the tunnel. He rounded the corner cautiously and then froze. There was yet another turn just up ahead, and he could detect a faint glimmer of light spilling into the passageway.

As Bolan took a step forward, the light suddenly went out and he could hear movement. He instinctively dropped to a crouch and leaned to one side. Seconds later, there were blips of light at the far end of the tunnel as a gun went off, shattering tiles on the wall behind Bolan. He quickly whipped his gun around and fired back.

It was difficult to hear anything over the echo of the gunshots, but Bolan strained his ears and detected the sound of retreating footsteps. He rose from his crouch and headed out, relying on memory to gauge the distance to the next bend. He stopped as he rounded the corner and listened hard. The footsteps were clearer now, and he guessed the gunman was fleeing down a straight stretch of tunnel. Switching his Beretta's firing mode to full-auto, Bolan took aim at the darkness and squeezed off the rest of his magazine in a sweeping spray.

There was no return fire.

As he moved slowly forward, the warrior quietly reached into his coat pocket for another clip. Nothing. Somehow he'd lost his replacement magazine while climbing down into the tunnel.

He wasn't about to turn back, however. Holstering the Beretta, he advanced. At one point he realized he was passing an intersection between two tunnels, and he again dropped to a crouch, wary that his foe might have managed to duck clear of the fusillade. When all remained still and silent, he continued forward. Three steps later he kicked something lying in the middle of the tunnel. He bent over, groping the floor until his fingers closed around the object.

A flashlight.

He turned it on, aiming its beam in the same direction he'd fired his Beretta moments before.

Suddenly Bolan heard a sound behind him. He whirled, bringing up the flashlight to illuminate a figure who'd just stepped out into the junction the warrior had passed earlier. The guy had his finger on the trigger of a .357 Magnum, aimed at Bolan's face.

"You're a dead man," Scotty Sear told the Executioner.

9

In one rapid movement, Bolan flicked off the flashlight and leaped to his right as the blast of gunfire echoed through the tunnel. He collided with the wall, his shoulder absorbing most of the blow. Dropping to a crouch, he clutched the flashlight tightly in his fist, waiting in the darkness for Sear's next move.

As it turned out, the biker's next move was to slump forward, landing face-first with a meaty thud on the tunnel floor. His gun fell from his grasp and skidded across the concrete to Bolan's feet. The warrior reached down and grabbed the weapon, uncertain as to what had happened?

"Belasko?" a familiar voice called out of the darkness.

Bolan raised his flashlight and cast its beam down the length of tunnel he'd just traversed. Nothing.

"Sheriff?" he said as he shifted the Magnum into his right hand.

Hough stepped out into the tunnel junction, holding his service revolver. As he glanced down at Sear's inert body, he said, "Guess I got him, huh?"

The Executioner shone his light on Sear, who was lying facedown on the ground, blood oozing from the entrance wound between his shoulder blades. Bolan checked for a pulse. There wasn't one.

"Yeah, you got him, all right. And not a moment too soon."

"Hell, just a lucky shot."

Bolan glanced up at the sheriff. "I wasn't expecting you down here."

"Neither was I," Hough confessed. "But I figured if you could wander down here looking for bogeymen, the least I could do was bring up the rear."

"I owe you one," Bolan told the other man.

Hough shrugged. "I'm a lawman, Belasko, not a loan shark. You don't owe me a thing."

The two men regarded each other with a newfound respect. Neither, however, found it necessary to voice his change of heart. The moment was acknowledged silently, then they turned their attention back to matters at hand. As Bolan turned Sear onto his back, Hough looked the dead man over.

"Know him?" Bolan asked.

"Yeah." Hough pointed to an insignia on the shoulder of the biker's coat. "Scotty Sear. Top dog for the Renegades. That's the same outfit that tried to take out you and Helena this morning."

The warrior nodded. "I wonder where they fit in with all this."

"Well, offhand," Hough surmised, "I'd guess Scotty here's behind the missing bodies."

"The whole family?"

"Yeah. They were all buried side by side, so once they tapped into one grave, there was no problem getting to the others."

Bolan frowned. "But how could he have known one of the tunnels ran so close to the graves?"

"Don't know," Hough said as he frisked Sear's pockets. Inside the dead man's coat were a couple pieces of folded paper. "Maybe this'll help."

Bolan shined his flashlight on the papers as Hough unfolded them. One sheet was an old blueprint of the Farthing Meadows Sanatorium facility, showing not only the buildings but also the layout of the underground tunnels. The second sheet was tracing paper, penciled in with just enough detail to suggest the boundaries of the present-day cemetery.

"A template," Bolan suggested.

"Yeah, I think you're right." Hough laid the tracing paper on top of the blueprint, matching borders, then pointing at a row of oblong boxes in the middle of the top sheet. "These are the graves. All they had to do was break into the tunnels and pinpoint their position, then dig away. What I want to know is why. What could the Renegades want with the bodies?"

"My guess is they didn't want the autopsies. And if that's the case, and given the way they went after me and Helena, I'd say they must have had something to do with the killings."

"Yeah, that would make sense, all right," Hough said. "But it still doesn't add up."

Bolan stood, making sure the magnum's safety was switched off. "Let's look around and see what else we can find out. Maybe the bodies are still down here somewhere."

"And maybe some of Sear's playmates are, too," Hough cautioned. He looked over the blueprint, noting pencil marks on the tunnel areas. He pointed to one of them. "My guess is this is where they got in. It's way back in the cemetery where they haven't developed any grave sites yet."

"Let's check it out."

The two men backtracked to the intersection and headed down the length of tunnel Bolan had bypassed shortly before being surprised by Sear. At the risk of telegraphing their approach, Bolan kept the flashlight on but pointed it low, just ahead of their feet. There were numerous footprints on the grime-covered concrete, most of them recent. The warrior motioned for them to pause for a closer look.

"At least two sets, maybe three," he whispered. "He definitely wasn't alone."

"Just what I wanted to hear," Hough muttered.

They proceeded down the tunnel. In the dim light it was easier to see the state of decay that had settled in on the passageway since its initial use. Mold and fungus clung to the tile walls, and there were sections where bits of the roof had collapsed, leaving mounds of dirt and broken tile on the floor. Light fixtures were built into the wall at regular intervals, but most of the bulbs were shattered.

After another fifty yards, the tunnel veered. Bolan switched off his flashlight when he and Hough saw a bright glow emanating from a room at the far end of the shaft. Enough illumination reached down the tunnel to light their way as they quietly padded forward.

They could hear activity in the room, the treading of feet, the clatter of metal stands, the faint chinking of glass and the hiss of a kerosene lamp. The noise helped to mask Bolan's and Hough's approach, and soon they were crouched less than three feet from the opening. Both men readied their weapons in two-hand grips, then Bolan nodded off a three-count.

On the third not, both men bolted into the doorway, swinging their guns into firing position.

"Freeze!" Hough commanded. "Police."

Inside the room was another member of the Renegades, bearded with his long dark hair pulled back in a ponytail and his arms wrapped around a huge cardboard box filled with glass beakers, scales and other paraphernalia. He eyed Bolan and Hough with wary disbelief.

"Shit," he gasped. "Don't shoot, man!"

"Put the box down," Bolan told him. "Slowly."

"Okay, okay, but don't shoot. I'm not armed."

The biker crouched slightly as he eased the box to the floor. As he stepped back from it, his hand went to his waist. Bolan saw a telltale glint of gunmetal and fired his Beretta. The Renegade took a 3-shot blast in the chest and reeled backward, dropping the gun he'd pulled from his pants. He was dead by the time he landed on the floor.

"Not armed, my ass," Hough said as he stepped forward, picking up the dead man's gun, a monstrous .454 Casull.

Along one wall of the chamber was a concrete staircase leading up to the surface. Bolan bounded up the steps, calling out to Hough, "There must be somebody else."

"Careful you don't wander into an ambush," Hough warned.

The heavy wooden doors that normally sealed off the staircase were open, and Bolan could see sky poking through the trees as he headed up the steps. He took the sheriff's advice to heart, slowing down the closer he got to the surface. If there was anyone outside the entrance, he would have undoubtedly heard the altercation below and be waiting, most likely armed with something at least as deadly as the slain Renegade's Casull.

Resting on one of the upper steps was a large sack filled with a white powder. Bolan doubted it was cocaine. More likely it was lactose or some other substance that would be used to cut the coke before it hit the street. He had a different use in mind for the bag, however.

Leaning over, he carefully hefted the powder, all the while straining his ears for any sounds of activity on the surface. Beyond the twittering of birds and the rustle of leaves, there was nothing.

"We've got people outside waiting for you," he called out. "Put the gun down and get your hands in the air!"

He waited a moment. Hearing no response, he continued up the steps, hurling the bag through the opening ahead of him. As he'd hoped, the bag drew fire, and when Bolan emerged right behind it, he'd gained a few seconds on his would-be assailant and was able to spot him before he became targeted.

The gunman was leaning over the back of a pickup truck, hands clasped around a cheap Saturday night Special. As he drew aim on Bolan, a 9 mm parabellum round caught him in the face, snapping his head back. His gun fired aimlessly into the truck's bed, then he keeled over into the dirt.

As Bolan looked around to make sure there were no other Renegades about, Hough emerged from the underground as well. As the sheriff had explained, this was a remote section of the cemetery, well concealed from view of any mourners or the people still assembled at the Simmonses' grave site.

Bolan stepped slowly through the white cloud of powder rising from the bag on the ground and approached the pickup. A quick glance into the back yielded no sign of the missing bodies. However, there was a second set of tire tracks next to where the slain Renegade lay. The sheriff joined him and followed the tracks with his eyes.

"Whatever they were using for a hearse, they got away. Damn."

Deal Yourself In and Play
GOLD EAGLE'S
ACTION POKER

A♠

Peel
off
this card
and complete
the hand
on the
next
page

It could get you:

♠ 4 Free books

♠ PLUS a free surprise gift

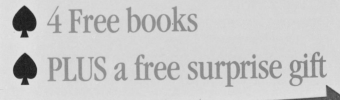

PLAY "ACTION POKER" AND GET . . .

★ 4 Hard-hitting, action-packed Gold Eagle novels — FREE

★ PLUS a surprise mystery gift — FREE

Peel off the card on the front of this brochure and stick it in the hand opposite. Find out how many gifts you can receive ABSOLUTELY FREE. They're yours to keep even if you never buy another Gold Eagle novel!

THEN DEAL YOURSELF IN FOR MORE GUT-CHILLING ACTION AT DEEP SUBSCRIBER SAVINGS

1. Play Action Poker as instructed on the opposite page.

2. Send back the card and you'll get hot-off-the-press Gold Eagle books, never before published. These books have a total cover price of $16.98, but they are yours to keep absolutely free.

3. There's no catch. You're under no obligation to buy anything. We charge nothing — ZERO — for your first shipment. And you don't have to make any minimum number of purchases — not even one!

4. The fact is thousands of readers enjoy receiving books by mail from the Gold Eagle Reader Service. They like the convenience of home delivery...they like getting the best new novels before they're available in stores...and they think our discount prices are dynamite!

5. We hope that after receiving your free books you'll want to remain a subscriber. But the choice is yours — to continue or cancel, anytime at all! So why not take us up on our invitation, with no risk of any kind. You'll be glad you did!

AND THERE'S MORE!!!

- With every shipment you'll receive *AUTOMAG,* our exciting newsletter — FREE.

SO DON'T WAIT UNTIL YOUR FAVORITE TITLES HAVE BEEN SNAPPED UP! YOU GET CONVENIENT FREE DELIVERY RIGHT TO YOUR DOOR. AT DEEP DISCOUNTS. GIVE US A TRY!

SURPRISE MYSTERY GIFT COULD BE YOURS <u>FREE</u> WHEN YOU PLAY ACTION POKER

The Executioner turned his attention to the back of the truck. In addition to shovels and a power generator, it held several boxes filled with equipment similar to that down in the stairwell.

"They must have had a drug lab here," he said.

"Makes sense," Hough agreed, coming over and peering into one of the boxes. "The Renegades are big suppliers in these parts."

Bolan picked up one of the glass beakers and held it to the light.

"What are you looking for?" Hough asked.

"Here, have a look for yourself.

The sheriff squinted his eyes, staring at the underside of the beaker.

"'Property of Gerley Chemical Company,'" he read. "Well, what do you know...."

10

Tim Jeffler had been smuggling classified information and other Gerley Chemical materials to the outside for the better part of three months, ever since getting a job in the company's waste-management operations. He got the position in part due to the letters of recommendation from his brother and a few other people at Sanicorp, where he'd worked the previous three years.

Some of the time, like today, he'd merely secreted items inside mismarked fifty-gallon drums being picked up by Sanicorp as part of their routine waste disposal. Other times, when he got his hands on papers small enough to fit smaller containers, he'd made drops on his lunch break. He was close friends with a couple of the men working internal security and had thus far been able to stay one step ahead of their attempts to squash plant espionage. But now it seemed as if they were starting to catch up with him, and he was on the verge of panic.

"I can't make any more outside drops," he told his brother. "It's too damn risky."

Todd Jeffler nodded, maintaining a cool facade. "I understand."

"They're really cracking down here," Tim went on, swallowing hard. "I don't even know how much longer I can get away with slipping stuff into the waste bins."

"Look, take it easy, Tim, will you?" Todd whispered, glancing up at a security camera viewing the dock area from its perch in the rafters. "You're going to blow this whole thing open on your own if you don't watch out."

The brothers were standing next to a bank of vending machines near the loading dock. There was no one else around, allowing them to speak freely. In the background, one of the other plant workers checked clearance as Pedro Billings used a forklift to hoist the drums of toxic waste into the back of the Sanicorp truck.

Tim steadied his hands as he sipped from a foam cup of coffee. But Todd could still see the fear in his brother's eyes.

"There's word going around that somebody got shot by the parking lot last night," Tim said, "near the drop site. Do you know anything about that?"

Todd briefly debated whether to fill Tim in, then decided against it. His brother was too skittish, and it wasn't worth the risk of pushing him over the edge. "Yeah, I heard about it," he said, concocting a cover story. "Some transient jumped this couple down by the river, and things got a little out of hand. Nothing to do with this."

"Still, I can't do any more of those drops," Tim insisted. "If I can still get access to R and D, I'll try to slip stuff in with the wastes, but I can't make any—"

"Tim, Tim. It's all right, okay?"

"I mean, I need the extra money and everything, but it's—"

"Don't worry about the money," Todd assured him. "It'll keep coming in, even if we lay low for a while."

"You're sure?"

The deputy nodded, offering his brother a tight smile. "Got to make sure we keep your mouth shut, right?"

"Hey, that's a given," Tim said. "Come on, you know me...."

Todd finished his coffee and crushed the cup, then tossed it into a nearby trash bin. "I got to go, bro. Hang in there." He gave Tim a light slap on the cheek. "And lighten up, okay? Go home and have a few beers tonight. Watch the ball game, have Stacie drop by for a little in-out."

"Yeah." Tim laughed. It sounded forced. "Yeah, good idea."

As the men headed across the dock, Todd Jeffler let out a slow breath. He was worried about Tim. The guy was definitely spooked, and as such he posed a possible risk to the operation. That wasn't good, especially the way things were going. If Tim was anyone else,

Todd would arrange a little "accident" that would silence him before he had a chance to muck things up. As it was, the deputy knew he was going to have trouble keeping Tosca, Cerdae, or anyone else from catching wind of Tim's state of mind and taking matters into their own hands.

Billings backed the forklift out of the truck and parked it, then fell into step beside the Jeffler brothers.

"We all set?" Todd asked.

"Bingo," Pedro told him.

"Okay, then let's hit it." He turned to his brother. "Maybe I'll swing by for the game later."

"Sounds good," Tim said.

Jeffler and Billings got back into the truck and pulled away from the loading dock. At the main gate they stopped the truck but left it running. As was customary, a team of security guards conducted a quick inspection of the vehicle, checking its cargo against an inventory bill of lading. Because all the drums were safety-sealed and marked as hazardous wastes, nobody was about to crack them open for a closer look.

When the inspection was finished, Jeffler and Billings turned in their visitor IDs and got back into the truck. Pulling away from the facility, they took the bridge over Long Noise River, then turned onto Birti Avenue, a two-lane road that ran past the trailer-home park. Glancing out his window, Jeffler could just see the blackened room of Ken Bridony's trailer.

As they drove on, Billings casually asked, "What's with your brother?"

"What do you mean?"

"Seemed a little antsy, didn't he?"

Jeffler shrugged. "Yeah, but you'd probably be antsy too if your girlfriend was a week late with her period."

"Oh, man," Billings groaned. "Shit, yes, I'd be one shook up son of a bitch."

Four miles down the road, they were in open country. They passed the Simmons farm, set back off the road, lying untended since the recent murders. Jeffler's hands tightened on the steering wheel as he eyed the property. He'd driven past the farm countless times since the killings, and each time he felt a cold chill travel the length of his spine. There was no way he could look at the house and not recall the innocent look on the faces of the sleeping Simmons children that night, when he and Tosca had roamed from room to room, determined to finish the killing spree that had begun when they'd gunned down Joey Simmons out by the creek behind the barn.

Jeffler turned onto a small dirt road just beyond the farm. He drove past more open fields, crossing a bridge that spanned the small creek.

Three miles in, the deputy pulled the truck off the road, following twin ruts that led through a forest of ancient oak trees. Once the vehicle was beyond sight of the dirt road, Jeffler killed the engine.

The men got out and circled to the back of the truck, opening the doors. Using a hydraulic lift, they lowered the first of the fifty-gallon drums to the ground.

"Okay, let's suit up," Jeffler said as soon as he had leaped off the truck.

After donning their protective gear except for the masks, the men tipped the drum on its side and rolled it through the leaves until they came to a ditch left by a dried stream. Although the rest of the ground was relatively dry, the base of the ditch was muddy and discolored.

"Hey, look over there," Billings said, gesturing a few yards to the right of the ditch, where the rotting carcass of a deer lay exposed to the elements, covered with flies and half-eaten by predators.

"Tough break, Bambi," Jeffler drawled.

"Yeah." Billings laughed. "Must have been something it drank."

The men went back for more barrels, then slipped on their safety masks. Setting the barrels upright, they carefully cracked the safety seals, then slowly tipped them forward, emptying their liquid wastes into the ditch. Some of it was in sludge form, while other drums poured more easily. It took a little over half an hour to drain all but one of the containers, in the process creating a murky, foul-smelling pool at the base of the ditch.

"Kind of makes you want to go skinny dipping, huh?" Jeffler joked as they eyed their handiwork.

"Yeah, after you," Billings said. "Come on, let's empty that last sucker, then load these back up and get out of here."

"No, we're already done," Jeffler told him.

"But what about that other—"

"I'll take care of that one personally," the deputy assured the biker.

"Fine by me."

After they reloaded the drums into the truck, the men used rakes to toss a thin layer of leaves over the spill.

"Okay," Jeffler pronounced once he raked a last load of leaves into place. "So much for state-of-the-art waste disposal."

They got into the truck and pulled away, leaving the toxic residue to seep its way slowly into the Michigan soil.

"WHAT I CAN'T FIGURE OUT is how a biker gang would get its hands on blueprints for an insane asylum that was demolished a couple decades ago," Grimaldi said to Bolan as he tugged the joystick and his Bell helicopter rose into the air over Farthing Meadows Cemetery.

"Hopefully we'll be able to find out soon enough." Bolan stared down at Sheriff Hough, who was huddled with the coroner and the paramedics who had shown up to deal with the three slain members of the Renegades. The Executioner had patched through a call requesting that Grimaldi pick him up in a chopper. Their objective was simple: to reach the Renegades' isolated compound before the bikers received word that their leader and two more members had been gunned down at the cemetery. State police would be converging on the site within the hour, but Bolan wanted to get there first.

"Helena came to about an hour ago," Grimaldi reported as they made their way northward, passing over the glitter of several small bodies of water, including Lake Jeltz.

"She okay?"

"Yeah, she's fine. You don't go through everything she's had to deal with the past month without getting tough. The doctor said she'd need more time to recuperate before we put her through any more questioning, though."

"Makes sense," Bolan said. "But it might be worthwhile if we could just get her okay to access her notes on that magazine piece she did about Gerley Chemical a couple months back."

"You think it has some bearing on all this?"

"It has to, if only incidentally."

"How do you mean?"

"She was looking at a completely different set of problems than we are," Bolan explained. "She might have come across information that had no bearing on her story but ties right into what we're looking for."

"Okay, I see what you're getting at. We sure as hell could use some kind of breakthrough."

"I take it you haven't turned up anything else on Bridony."

Grimaldi shook his head. "At least nothing solid. I checked out a few places he worked at prior to his job with Joey Simmons. No problems. And nobody at the trailer park remembers noticing anything unusual about him. He just kind of came and went. If somebody waved to him, he'd wave back, but that's about as much as he got involved with anyone there."

"What about the school?"

"Well, funny you should ask,," the Stony Man pilot said, gesturing out the window. "There it is, just off the east shore of that big lake."

He banked the chopper to the right, casting its shadow across the choppy waters of Lake Jeltz.

As they drifted over the campus of the Beta Institute, Bolan said, "Looks pretty well kept up."

"Cleanest place I've been to since Disneyland. I talked to one of the administrators, and he said most of the live-ins do grounds work and other manual labor to help pay their expenses."

"Sounds a little like a chain gang to me," Bolan said.

"Sort of, but I got the idea everybody seemed to enjoy themselves a little more. Too much, if you ask me."

"What do you mean?"

Grimaldi shrugged. "Well, the few people I saw out on the grounds had this real blissed-out look. You know, like they'd spent a little too much time staring at their navels."

"But what about Bridony?" Bolan asked, getting back to the issue at hand.

"Their records confirmed he was taking an adult education class on computer programming. Paid in cash and had a good attendance record. I wasn't able to get in touch with the instructor or any of the students. Other than that, I came up with zip."

As they flew over the main entrance, Bolan took a close look at one of the guards standing outside the security shack. "Hold on. You see the firepower that guy's packing?"

Grimaldi nodded. "First thing I noticed when I pulled up. They said it's a precaution against some of the teens in the detox wing. Apparently they get out of hand once in a while and either try to run away or make trouble for the other students. The guns are only loaded with rubber bullets, though... or at least that's what I was told."

Bolan frowned, continuing to stare at the grounds as they pulled away. "It doesn't add up right for me somehow."

"I know what you mean. I think tackling the Renegades is our best bet now, but at some point we ought to take a closer look."

"I agree."

They left the campus behind and headed out over farmland. The radio crackled to life. It was Brognola calling from Mosenan Isle. He reported that Able

Team had just arrived on the island and would be spearheading security at the infirmary for as long as Helena was hospitalized.

"Glad to hear it," Bolan said. He went on to ask about securing the notes to Helena's magazine articles about Gerley Chemical and any other local activities that might tie in to the crisis.

"Good idea," Brognola replied. "I'll broach the subject with her once her doctor gives the green light."

"One other thing," Bolan suggested before signing off. "When you check in with the Farm, you might want to have Bear run a computer check on Farthing Meadows back when it was an asylum. See if there's any link at all with Gerley Chemical."

"Consider it done."

Bear was Aaron Kurtzman, Stony Man Farm's wheelchair-bound communications expert and resident computer whiz. Like Grimaldi and weaponsmith John Kissinger, the Bear was an indispensable cog in the Farm's operations. Able to tap into data bases of more than five hundred different universities and government think tanks, as well as nearly every intelligence agency in the States and several abroad, Kurtzman could be counted on to not only assimilate a wealth of information on any given topic, but also organize, condense and evaluate it, usually in half the time any team of professional hackers and programmers could.

Sheriff Hough had provided Bolan with the location of the Renegades' back-country compound, and as the chopper neared its destination, Bolan and Grimaldi plotted strategy. The Executioner was in favor of setting down a quarter mile from the headquarters and going the rest of the way on foot. The pilot had other ideas.

"We'd lose all the time we've gained by flying up here," he reasoned, "and if they've got their perimeter staked out, we're going to get bogged down trying to punch our way through."

Bolan glanced at his friend. "You want to fly in?"

"Hell, why not? It wouldn't be the first time I've gone behind enemy lines. And it's not like these guys are going to have antiaircraft guns or anything."

"No, but if they have any more of these, they could do some serious damage," Bolan said, glancing down at the .454 Casull he'd appropriated from one of the fallen bikers. The Casull was relatively new to the market but had already supplanted the .44 Magnum as the world's most powerful handgun. Housing bullets so huge that only five could be crammed into the gun's chunky cylinder, the Casull fired with a muzzle velocity of two thousand feet per second, double that of the Magnum. There were numerous cases of unprepared owners of this brute of a weapon winding up in the hospital with broken wrists because they underestimated the back kick. John Kissinger had perhaps best explained the gun after testing it back at the Farm's shooting range, calling it half-donkey, half-midget howitzer.

"I say we take our chances," Grimaldi said. "It's not like they're expecting us. And don't forget, we've already thinned their ranks. So what do you say? Do we go for it?"

Bolan nodded. "Yeah. Let's go for it."

"All right!" Grimaldi shoved the joystick forward, dipping the Bell forward. "Ready or not, here we come..."

11

"Look, I know you're upset, Doc," Rosey Tosca said, "but I'm trying to help you out here."

Dr. Dykes glanced up from his desk, his eyes dark with smoldering anger and frustration. "What business of yours is it what happens to the patients I lose?"

"I'm sure you run some tests, try to find out what went wrong and all that," Tosca forged on, pacing the doctor's office, a spacious room with a view of the lake. "But at some point you have to get rid of the bodies, right? And what do you do? Do you bury them?"

"I don't owe you an explanation."

"You do, don't you? You bury them, probably somewhere here on the property, where they can turn up as evidence at some point down the line."

Tosca knew he'd touched a nerve. He fell silent and turned his back on the doctor, pretending to busy himself looking out at the activity on the lake. He could see Dykes's reflection in the window, and after a moment the doctor rose from his chair.

"Why are you bringing this up?" Dykes asked, an edge of menace lurking behind the casual tone in his voice. "Are we talking about blackmail here? Is that it?"

Tosca forced a laugh and turned back to face the doctor. "You're paranoid, Doc. No, I'm not talking about blackmail. I'm talking about getting rid of your mistakes…getting rid of them in a way that they can't come back to haunt you."

"I see." Dykes moved out from around the desk, pressing the fingertips of one hand against those of the other. "And you're offering to do this out of the goodness of your heart."

Tosca shook his head. "Hell, no. It'll cost you, but it'll be worth it, too."

"How much?" Dykes wanted to know.

"I'll leave that to your judgment. You've always been fair with me before."

"I'm pleased to hear that," Dykes said, walking to the door. As he held it open, he told Tosca, "Let me think about this. I can have an answer for you tomorrow."

"Fine." Tosca shook the doctor's hand and left the office. Heading to the elevator, he beamed. Nice move, he assured himself. He knew he'd won Dykes over, and if previous experience was any judge, by letting the doctor name his price, Tosca was sure he'd end up with a better deal than he might have proposed on his own. And, by endearing himself further to Dykes, he'd become privy to more and more information about operations at the institute. That could always come in handy, in a number of respects, not the least of which was the fact that a wealth of incriminating evidence could come in handy in a worst-case scenario, should Tosca ever find himself on the wrong side of the law and forced into a position of cutting a deal with the D.A. The more he knew about Dykes, the more likely he would walk away from any court situation with immunity from prosecution. It was a no-lose situation, Tosca figured, and he was feeling full of himself for having orchestrated it.

But, of course, there were still countless other machinations to tend to.

Leaving the laboratory, the hardman got in his car and picked up his cellular phone. He wanted to make sure Jeffler had made his pickup at Gerley Chemical. Thumbing through his personal directory, Tosca dialed a number that put him in touch with Jeffler in the Sanicorp delivery truck. The deputy didn't sound happy to be hearing from him.

"What do you want?" Jeffler asked.

"Hey, lighten up, Toddster," Tosca told the other man. "Did you have some kind of problem?"

"Not really. What about you? You get your chores taken care of?"

Tosca didn't reply at first. He hadn't received confirmation from either Brewster or Sear yet, so he couldn't be sure whether Helena Simmons had been taken out or if the bodies of her brother and his family had been removed from the cemetery. He decided to put Jeffler off for the moment. "I'll tell you about it later. Where are you now?"

Jeffler reported that he'd just finished dumping a load of wastes from Gerley Chemical and was on his way to make a delivery to the Beta Institute.

"Small world," Tosca told the deputy. "That's where I'm calling from."

"Yeah?"

"Yeah. Dr. Dykes was playing mad scientist and I wanted to catch the matinee performance."

"How'd it go?"

"Man puts on quite a show," Tosca answered cryptically.

"Well, I've got your stuff, too," Jeffler said. "You want to just stay put and pick it up there?"

Tosca checked his watch. "How far away are you?"

"I don't know, about twenty minutes or so."

"Okay, sure. I'll wait."

As soon as Tosca got off the phone with Jeffler, he tried calling Brewster and Sear. There was no answer at Brewster's apartment, and he wasn't at the Renegades' compound, either. Nobody had heard from him all day, but Tosca knew that Brewster didn't spend that much time at the headquarters, so it wasn't necessarily anything to be worried about. As for Sear, Jeffler was told that he'd taken off with a few other members of the gang at least five hours earlier, supposedly on some hush-hush errand. Tosca figured that errand undoubtedly involved raiding the graves at Farthing Meadows Cemetery. Again, it was a case of no news being nothing more than that—no news. He assured himself that everything had gone smoothly, but as he got out of the car, he couldn't help but feel a certain vague uneasiness.

"Easy, Rosey," he told himself. "Don't psyche yourself out here. Everything's going smooth. Nice and smooth."

Strolling away from the laboratory complex, Tosca roamed the grounds, steering clear of those areas he knew from previous experience were off-limits. He could see guards discreetly posted about the campus, maintaining a low profile as they kept an eye on him and the scattered groups of students. Tosca knew that schedules at the institute were carefully structured in such a way that off-campus students would have access to the grounds to attend conventional classes at a time when the imprisoned residents were safely out of sight, either in underground classrooms or in housing facilities on the far side of campus. Such an arrangement allowed for the campus to retain an aura of relative credibility in the eyes of the outside community while still ensuring enough privacy to conduct more questionable programs.

There was a cafeteria with outdoor seating next to the largest of the classroom buildings. Tosca bought a bottle of fruit juice, then sat down to drink it a few tables away from a handful of students who were in the midst of a fervent discussion about anthropology. They were all clear-eyed and articulate, and Tosca was certain at first that they were off-campus students, but then he took a closer look and recognized the girl he'd abused back in the lab an hour earlier. She showed no signs of having been recently sedated, and when she inadvertently met Tosca's gaze, there was no hint of recognition in her gaze.

Tosca wasn't sure what to make of it. After seeing the flower boy die so unexpectedly while talking to his "counselor" in the lab, he'd had his doubts about the success of Dr. Dykes's experiments, but here was this young woman carrying on a lucid conversation about anthropology, apparently oblivious to the degradations Tosca had subjected her to only a short time ago.

Before Tosca could dwell further on the matter, he spotted the Sanicorp truck heading across campus. He quickly finished his drink and started back, reaching the garage above the laboratory just as Jeffler was preparing to off-load the one fifty-gallon drum he and Pedro Billings hadn't emptied into the woods. Billings was nowhere around; Jeffler had dropped him off at the Renegades' compound.

"Just a second," Tosca called out, striding past one of the guards and climbing into the back of the parked truck.

"What's the matter?" Jeffler wanted to know.

Tosca tapped the drum. "Is my stuff in here?"

"Yeah. I was going to give it to you after we delivered Dykes's shake."

"I've got a better idea," the hardman said. "Why don't you crack this sucker open and give me my share now. No sense in Dykes having to know about it, right?"

Jeffler thought it over, then nodded. "That's fine by me."

The deputy took out a set of keys and unlocked the two different sets of metal bands tightly bound around the drum. "So," he said as he loosened the bands, "what's the bottom line with Helena? Did you get rid of her or not?"

There was no way Tosca could avoid an answer this time. "I'm still waiting to hear."

"What do you mean, waiting to hear?" The deputy was incredulous. "Did you do it or not?"

"Look, I had some other things to tend to, all right?" Tosca snapped. "I put Brewster on it."

"Brewster?"

"That's right!" Tosca said. "And Scotty Sear's taking care of the bodies, so don't go blowing a gasket."

Jeffler shook his head with disgust. "Typical. Rope some other sucker into doing your work for you."

"Kiss my ass. Who do you think risked his neck to have Ken Bridony take the fall for those killings? I didn't see you nearly getting blown to bits setting that trailer on fire, did I?"

"Okay, so one time you—"

Tosca leaned into Jeffler, pressing him against the wall of the truck. They faced off, eye-to-eye. "Look here, Deputy. I pull my weight in this operation, and I don't need you hiding behind big Frankie and trying to tell me I don't." He pulled out his gun and pressed the barrel on the underside of Jeffler's chin. "You want to see me take somebody out? Is that what you want to see?''

"Easy, man," Jeffler whispered, glancing down at the gun in Tosca's hand. "I was just—"

"I know what you were doing. Trying to put me in my place, right?"

"No, look, I just asked you a question," Jeffler said. "That's all, okay? I asked you a question and you gave me an answer. We're all squared away. No problem."

Tosca kept the gun pressed against the deputy's throat a moment longer, then pulled it away. The rage left his face, replaced by a calm smile. "No problem," he repeated. "That's good. That's real good. Then where were we?"

"I was getting the stuff for you to bring to the Bolivians tonight," Jeffler told him, moving back over to the sealed drum. No one had witnessed their altercation, and in a way the deputy was disappointed. A part of him wished that one of the guards had spotted Tosca and gunned him down. It would have made things a little easier. As it was, though, Jeffler would have to play along with his sometime partner. At least for now.

As Jeffler peeled the straps off the barrel, Tosca wondered aloud, "Hey, don't I need to put a special suit on or something?"

"No. Everything inside's super sealed. I mean, you could pack eggs in there and drop them from an eight-story building and they wouldn't break."

"That's a comfort."

"You're damn right it is," Jeffler replied.

Once the straps were unlocked, Tosca and the deputy carefully pried the lid off the drum. Inside, sandwiched between thick pads of foam, were two elongated cylinders approximately seven inches in diameter and sixteen inches long. One of the cylinders contained a variety of chemicals Dr. Dykes had requested for use in his ongoing experiments.

The other cylinder contained separately packed vials that contained samples of the different biological- and chemical-warfare agents that Gerley Chemical was under contract to develop antidotes and early detection systems for. In addition to mustard gas and a solution containing the anthrax-causing microbe *bacillus anthracis,* there were also tubes of tabun and sarin, nerve gases created by Nazi Germany for use in the concentration camps of World War Two. In all, there was perhaps a total of six ounces of fluid in the various containers. To the uneducated, it might have seemed like an insignificant amount, but both Tosca and the people he was dealing with knew that placed in the right hands, combined with the right weapons systems and unleashed under the right circumstances, those six ounces could be capable of killing the entire population of a city the size of Detroit.

"Okay," Tosca said once he had the second cylinder in his hands, "Time to bring on the Bolivians."

THE SIX-ACRE PARCEL of land that now served as home base for the Renegades bike club had originally been owned by the parents of John Brewster. They'd run a tree nursery on the site for more than thirty years before their untimely deaths in a car crash ten years earlier. As sole heir, Brewster had been deeded the property, and within six months the Renegades had moved in along with him. Most of the inventory was sold off to other nearby nurseries, but the various greenhouses and equipment sheds remained standing. Marijuana cultivation became the primary source of income for the group, but after numerous raids, the bikers got out of the manufacturing end of things and turned their attention to distribution. Instead of marijuana they dealt in more expensive trade, mostly cocaine but also a little crack and heroin. And instead of running the drugs through the nursery, they opted for more clandestine fronts, like Farthing Meadows Cemetery and a storage facility down the block from Mofo's.

Now, having received word of Brewster's death earlier that morning, the mood at the compound was decidedly downbeat. There was a little token mourning at the loss of a brother and a few scattered cries for retribution, but most of the members were concerned with more practical matters, such as the status of the property they were living on.

"I mean, it's not like Brewster wrote up a will or anything," Pedro Billings complained as he whittled a stick near one of the smaller greenhouses. He was sitting backward on his parked Harley, feet propped up on the sissy seat, tapping the chrome in time to the music blaring over a portable tape player.

Another of the bikers, Vince Henhill, sat on the steps leading up to the greenhouse, hand-rolling a joint. "What, you think somebody's going to come up with the balls to try to evict us?" Henhill lighted the joint and filled his lungs with smoke, then let it out in one long exhalation, laughing. "Sheeeeee-it, I'd like to see them try...."

Billings reached out for the joint, then leaned back for a hit. His eyes suddenly widened as he glanced above the nearby treetops.

"Don't look now, Henny," he told his cohort, "but it looks like that's just what they're about to do."

"Huh?" Henhill rose to his feet, hearing a high-pitched drone in the air for the first time. He reached over and turned off the music, then looked skyward, tracing the sound to the Bell helicopter. "Shit, man, they're going to land right in our front yard!"

"Maybe we better go lay out the red carpet," Billings said, tossing aside the stick he was whittling.

"You mean with their blood?"

"Hey, you're a regular Einstein, Henny," Billings drawled. He slipped his knife into a sheath strapped to his thigh, then climbed to the top of the steps, leaning inside the doorway. There was an intercom mounted to the door frame. He pressed it, establishing communication with the main house.

"Got ourselves some visitors, and I don't think they're friendlies."

The intercom speaker squawked, followed by a response from another biker. "We see them. Let's find out what they want before we jump into anything, though. You got that, Billings?"

"Yeah, I got it," Billings replied, sneering into the box, flashing his middle finger at the speaker. "Loud and clear."

He bounded down the steps and slid onto his bike. As he cranked the engine to life, he shouted to Henhill, "Come on!"

Henhill clambered onto the rear seat of the bike and planted his feet on pegs mounted to the Harley's frame. The shadow of the approaching helicopter swept past them, and when they looked up they could see the aircraft veering past the greenhouse as it continued to descend.

Billings opened the throttle and sped off in pursuit of the chopper. Henhill pulled a Detonics .45 pistol from a shoulder harness bulging beneath his denim vest.

"I've been waiting for a chance to break this baby in," he shouted into Billings's ear, his voice filled with expectation. "I'm going to drill some bastard full of holes!"

12

"I know this was my idea," Grimaldi said as he brought the Bell copter down over the Renegades' compound, "but maybe it would have been a better idea if we'd gotten our hands on a bird with a little more punch. You know, like an Apache."

"Nothing we can do about it now," Bolan said, slipping the Casull into his shoulder holster. As powerful as the gun was, he planned to use it only as a backup, preferring the familiarity and faster firing of his Beretta.

"I see plenty of bikes, but no trucks or station wagons," Grimaldi commented as he passed over the property. "You think maybe they haven't come back from the cemetery yet?"

"If they did, maybe they're parked in one of those sheds."

"Then again, maybe they took the bodies somewhere else and we're here on a wild-goose chase."

"I wouldn't go that far," the Executioner said, raising a pair of high-powered Bushnell binoculars to his eyes and scanning the property. "We already know they're into a whole lot more than grave robbing. We'll be able to nail them on something.''

''Of course, we did overlook a few details,'' Grimaldi reminded Bolan, ''like getting our hands on search warrants.''

''The state police'll have that covered,'' the warrior replied, directing his attention to the outer edges of the property. ''I count five cruisers about a quarter mile away.''

''Should we hold back and wait for them?''

''We're already here.'' Bolan quickly surveyed the heart of the compound, plotting their next move. ''Look, can you set down behind that ridge over there? Just long enough for me to get out.''

''Yeah, sure,'' Grimaldi said, eyeing the terrain and adjusting the Bell's course. ''Then what?''

''Then stay airborne and keep them distracted. I'll run a quick search of the buildings.''

''Keep them distracted,'' Grimaldi repeated. ''In other words, let them take pot shots at me.''

''There'll be state troopers swarming on them, too.''

''Fair enough.''

Grimaldi maneuvered the Bell over a row of elm trees. As they approached the ridge, both men heard and felt a bullet skim off the underside of the helicopter. Bolan glanced down and saw a Renegade standing next to one of the greenhouses, taking aim with what looked to be an M-16.

''Bank right!'' Bolan shouted.

The pilot jerked the controls, abruptly changing course. He averted a direct hit and slipped behind the cover of the ridge, but not before the M-16 took a bite out of the Bell's nose section.

"Close call," Grimaldi muttered as he set the aircraft down.

"Just the way you like it," Bolan said as he unstrapped himself and climbed out of the helicopter, flashing Grimaldi a thumbs-up before dropping to the ground. He hunched over to avoid the rotors, and as the Bell swung back up into the air, he stormed up the pitched slope of the ridge. Once he cleared the rise, he lay flat, lining his sights on the sniper next to the greenhouse.

The Renegade was concentrating on the copter, tracking its ascent with his M-16. Before he could get off his next shot, however, he was hammered by a triburst from Bolan's Beretta. Reeling to one side, he smashed one of the greenhouse panels with the rifle barrel, then slumped into the opening, impaling himself on a shaft of broken glass. By the time Bolan reached him, the biker was already dead, drenched in his own blood.

The Executioner reached behind his back and tucked the Beretta inside the waistband of his pants, then helped himself to the dead man's M-16.

Charging into the greenhouse, Bolan expected to find marijuana plants. To his surprise, however, he saw that the building had been converted into a workout room, complete with mismatched sets of weights, a Nautilus machine and a pool table. The glass at the far end of the chamber had been painted black to keep sunlight from spoiling the image on a huge 45-inch rear-projection TV screen. The television was tuned into a music video show, and the screen was filled with images of a heavy-metal band surrounded by panting nymphomaniacs in short skirts and spiked heels. Twin speakers on either side of the screen blared loudly as Bolan advanced, eyes open for anyone else who might be in the room.

There was a sudden blur of motion off to his right, and as Bolan turned, a pool ball bounded off the stock of his M-16 and slammed into his ribs. He grimaced from the impact as he ducked behind the Nautilus machine. Staring across the room, he spotted a Renegade reaching for a handgun resting on the edge of the pool table.

"Leave it there!" Bolan shouted.

The biker grabbed the gun and grunted as he tipped the heavy table on its side and dropped behind it for cover.

"All I want is information," Bolan called out. "You can walk out of here alive if—"

He was drowned out as the Renegade fired over the top of the table, flattening slugs against the stacked weights in the Nautilus machine. The warrior shifted the M-16 to his left hand and slowly withdrew the Casull from his holster with his right. He waited until he drew another round, then leaned out and returned fire. The pool table might have been thick enough to absorb rounds from nearly any other caliber hand-gun, but the Casull's .454 projectile punched easily through felt, slate and solid oak, and still retained enough velocity to burrow into the biker's chest. Dumbfounded, the Renegade dropped his gun and sprawled across the floor.

Bolan cautiously moved forward, making sure the biker didn't make another move for his gun. Once he was at the wounded man's side, he looked him in the eye and demanded, "Some of your guys were out at the cemetery a couple hours ago. They took some bodies. I want to know where they took them."

The biker craned his head slightly and stared back at Bolan with pleading eyes. "I don't know anything about a cemetery," he gasped. "Hey, man, I'm hurting real bad. You got to—"

The man coughed up blood and his head dropped back to the floor with a loud thwack. His eyes remained open, as did his mouth, which continued to spill more blood.

Bolan stepped over the body and found the controls for the television. He shut the set off, turning the room silent. As he headed for the back door, he could hear sirens in the distance, as well as the drone of Grimaldi's helicopter and sporadic blasts of gunfire.

The war was joined.

"QUIT WASTING AMMO," Pedro Billings shouted.

Henhill ignored the other biker and fired again. "Come on, goddamn it!" he shouted at the distant helicopter, which continued to bob and weave just beyond range of the man's .45. "Get down!"

They were behind the main house, where they'd joined forces with another three gang members. Billings was still astride his idling Harley, but Henhill had climbed off so he'd have a steadier aim. Billings finally reached over and grabbed his companion's wrist, giving it a sharp jerk.

"I said knock it off!"

Henhill looked at Billings with disbelief. "Hey, what's the big—"

"Listen!" Billings snapped.

Henhill fell silent and listened a moment. "Sirens."

"Not just that," Billings said. "I think I heard some shots back near the weight room, too."

"What do you make of it?" one of the other bikers asked.

"Beats me," Billings said, cupping his hand over his eyes to block the sun as he tracked Grimaldi's diversionary flight pattern. "But there's no sense staying clumped together and making it easier for them. Let's split up."

He didn't bother putting the matter to a vote. Revving the throttle on his Harley, Billings roared away from the house. Contrary to what he'd told the others, he had a pretty good idea why the authorities might be closing in. He figured they'd either finally made the link between the Renegades and Sanicorp's illegal dumping of toxic wastes, or else something had gone wrong at the cemetery and the drug lab had been discovered. Since Billings was involved in both enterprises, he wasn't about to let himself be taken into custody. If Henhill or any of the others wanted to go out in a blaze of glory, that was certainly their right. Billings was going to flee, to live to fight another day.

At first he headed down a dirt road leading to the greenhouse, but halfway there he changed course, crashing his Harley through a spindly thicket and into the most heavily wooded area of the compound. There was no way any squad cars would be able to pursue him, and the tree cover overhead was thick enough that even the helicopter would be hard-pressed to follow his movements. All he had to do was make his way deep into the heart of the forest, where the gang had set up a number of well-camouflaged bunkers with a siege such as this in mind. He could hide out there for a few days, then slip away.

What Billings hadn't counted on was being followed into the brush by the man he'd heard exchanging gunfire at the greenhouse.

As he was weaving his way through knee-high foliage and between mature trees, Billings heard the chatter of an M-16. Almost in the same instant, he could also hear and feel a stream of hot lead raking its way along the side of his Harley. The rear tire exploded and his leg suddenly turned to fire as a pair of bullets tore through it. Losing control of the vehicle, the biker slammed into a fallen tree trunk and was thrown over the handlebars. The Harley went airborne as well, crashing down next to him after he'd landed face-first on the ground. The bike bucked for a moment before the engine died, then toppled over onto Billings, crushing his hip and pinning him to the ground.

The pain was excruciating, but the Renegade was still conscious and able to move his upper body. Grimacing, he reached for his gun as he heard Bolan advancing toward him through the brush. The weapon, however, was sandwiched between Billings's thigh and the Harley's fuel tank. He tried to push the bike off him, but he had neither the strength nor leverage. Moments later, Bolan was standing over him.

"Looks like you could use some help," the Executioner said calmly. "You're in luck. So could I."

Billings swallowed hard, trying to block out the pain. "What do you want?"

"There was a family murdered near Talville about a month ago. What did your gang have to do with that?"

"I don't know what you're talking about," Billings said.

"Wrong answer." Bolan placed one foot on the frame of the Harley and leaned forward, pressing the bike harder against Billings's wounds, forcing the biker to let out a cry of pain. "Try again."

"Look, look, I'll talk, okay?"

Bolan eased his weight off the bike. "All right, talk."

"If I do, can we cut some kind of deal? You know, in court..."

"You're in court right now," Bolan told the man. "The deal's this... you talk, you live. Take it or leave it. Now what about the murders?"

"We didn't have anything to do with that. I swear. We just..."

"You just what?"

Billings winced as a flash of pain shot through him. "Come on, man, you're hurting me!"

"You don't know what hurt is yet," Bolan warned. "You just what?"

"We just dumped stuff near their property," he explained. "That was all. We didn't kill anybody. Or at least I didn't."

"Dumped?" Bolan asked. "Dumped what?"

"Stuff," Billings repeated. "You know, from the chemical plant."

"Gerley?"

"Yeah. We pick up the stuff they can't just toss out in the regular trash and we get rid of it."

"Wait a minute," Bolan said. "You expect me to believe Gerley just lets a bike gang come in and take away—"

"No, it's not like that. We're in on it with some other outfit. Sanicorp. It's all legit."

"Legit? Dumping toxic waste on some people's farmland is legit?"

"All right, so maybe we cut a few corners."

Bolan tugged the Harley off Billings, then grabbed the man's gun and tossed it aside.

"Who's behind Sanicorp?" the Executioner demanded. "Who brought you into their operations?"

"A couple guys," Billings muttered.

"Names."

"Tosca. Rosey Tosca."

The name meant nothing to Bolan. "Who else?"

"Todd Jeffler."

"Jeffler?" Bolan said. "Deputy with the Sheriff's Department."

Billings nodded. "Yeah. He works for Sanicorp on his day off."

Bolan thought back to earlier that morning, when Jeffler had walked him out of Hough's office. The warrior had told the deputy about going to pick up Helena. Jeffler had had plenty of time to call the Renegades to line up the attempted ambush near the cornfield.

At last the pieces were starting to fall together.

13

There had been a limited exchange of gunfire after the state police had stormed the compound, but once the surviving Renegades realized how much their numbers had dwindled, they had surrendered. They'd been hauled off into custody while their slain and wounded comrades were transported to Macomb County General Hospital for treatment or tagging in the morgue.

Bolan and Grimaldi stayed behind at the nursery, taking advantage of the warrants secured by the state police to search the premises for evidence relevant to the gang's drug activities and any possible involvement in the disappearance of the bodies from Farthing Meadows Cemetery. Surprisingly they found nothing of value connected to either activity. There were, however, some items that had a pertinent bearing on other matters, particularly in light of the disclosures made by Pedro Billings.

"There's a closet full of uniforms for some outfit called Sanicorp," one of the police officers reported as he came out of one of the back rooms of the main house. Bolan and Grimaldi were in the kitchen, methodically searching drawers and cabinets. Neither had divulged the Sanicorp connection yet, and both remained stone-faced at the revelation. As soon as the officer headed off to inspect one of the other bedrooms, Bolan turned to Grimaldi, holding up a notepad that had been lying next to the phone.

"A Sanicorp letterhead," he said. "With an address."

"Bingo. You figure they used one of their trucks to carry the bodies from the graveyard?"

"There's one way to find out."

The men quickly finished searching the kitchen, then headed out of the house. After exchanging a few words with the ranking state police officer, they started toward the helicopter. Before they could get aboard, they heard the honking of a car horn and turned around to see Sheriff Hough approaching in his police cruiser. Hough parked and was out of the car by the time the others caught up with him.

"What's this I heard about some biker pointing a finger at one of my deputies?" he demanded.

"It's Jeffler." Bolan went on to relate the gist of Billings's confession, particularly concerning Sanicorp's connection with both Gerley and the Simmons family. Hough listened silently, trying to make sense of it all.

"Then what you're saying is," he ventured, "you think the murders had something to do with illegal waste dumping on the Simmonses' property?"

"Yeah, and I think the bodies were stolen because the killers figured enough of the wastes had gotten into the Simmonses' drinking water and it'd show up in an autopsy and finger them.''

"And if Jeffler was in on the dumping, he probably took part in the killings, too," Hough said, his face reddening with a growing rage.

"Billings didn't say as much, but it seems a safe bet," Bolan acknowledged. "Along with a Rosey Tosca."

"I know all about Tosca," Hough said. "He's a real mixer."

"How do you mean?" Grimaldi asked.

"I mean, he's got his fingers in a lot of illegal pies. Gangs, drugs, the Mob, money laundering...you name it. What he does is stake out a little bit of action on all fronts so that if there's too much heat in one field he can always turn to something else. Look at him out of context and he's just a nickel-dime hood, but add up all the bits and pieces, though, and he's a major player."

"What's this guy look like?" Bolan asked.

"Average height, good build," Hough said.

"Sounds like he's the one I ran into back in the woods behind Gerley Chemical."

"Yeah, now that you mention it...."

"Why isn't he behind bars?" Bolan asked.

Hough shrugged. "Same reason Jimmy Bariggia and most other Mob chiefs aren't. He gets other people to do his dirty work most of the time, and when he steps in on his own, he's damn good about covering his tracks. Oh, we've hauled him in a few times, but he always gets out on technicalities.''

"Lawyers?"

"Of course. Same firm that handles Bariggia's people, which should tell you something."

"Well, we're on our way to Sanicorp," Bolan said. "Any luck and we'll find Jeffler and Tosca there, along with the bodies and enough evidence to put them both deep enough behind bars that they'll have to plea-bargain to use the bathroom."

"Is there room in that bird for another man?" Hough asked.

"No problem," Grimaldi replied.

"Good. Then count me in and let's get cracking!"

"Here's the address," Bolan said, showing Hough the notepad as they headed for the helicopter. "Do you know where that is?"

"Yeah, I do."

"Great."

The men climbed into the Bell. Grimaldi fired up the engine, and they all strapped themselves in.

"You guys can have dibs on Tosca," Hough said, adding with determination, "but Jeffler's mine."

TODD JEFFLER HAD NO interest in indulging himself in sexual activity at the Beta Institute. When he made his deliveries to Dr. Dykes, he preferred to be paid in cash, which suited Dykes fine.

"Fifteen, sixteen, seventeen thousand dollars," the doctor said, stacking bundles of hundred-dollar bills on his desk. He slid the pile across to Jeffler, smiling at the deputy. "There you are."

"Pleasure doing business with you, Doctor." Jeffler gathered up the money and placed it in the canister he'd used to deliver Dykes's shipment of stolen pharmaceuticals from Gerley Chemical. "As always."

"Before you go," Dykes said, "I was wondering if I could ask you a question."

"Fire."

"It's about Rosey Tosca."

"What about him?"

"Can he be trusted?"

Jeffler didn't have to think long on that one. "He can be trusted to look out for his best interests, I can tell you that much."

"I see."

"Why do you ask?"

Dykes nonchalantly pressed a button on his intercom as he moved away from his desk. "I need to get down to the laboratory. Let me walk you."

"Sure, fine."

In fact, however, Jeffler didn't like the way things were shaping up. If there was bad blood developing between Dykes and Tosca, it would only be a matter of time before Jeffler would find himself trapped in conflicting alliances, and the last thing he wanted was to make his life more complicated than it already was.

As the two men stepped out into the hallway, they were joined by Frankie Cerdae, who had come in response to Dykes's summons on the intercom.

"Frankie," Dykes said, "why don't you bring Todd up-to-date on our problems?"

As he fell into step between Jeffler and Dykes, Cerdae asked the deputy, "Have you been in touch with the station at all since this morning?"

"No, I was making the rounds for Sanicorp. Why?"

"Well, you know how last night we told Tosca to take care of Helena Simmons?"

"Yeah. I just talked to him about it. He said he palmed the job off on a couple Renegades."

"That's right," Cerdae said, "and they botched it."

Jeffler felt a sudden tightening in the pit of his stomach. "That son of a bitch."

"And that's not all," Cerdae went on. "I just found out the Renegades have been shut down."

"What do you mean?"

"I mean, not only was their compound raided, but there was also some kind of shoot-out at Farthing Meadows. Apparently they found the drug lab."

"I don't believe this!" As they reached the end of the hallway, the deputy lashed out, smacking his fist against the wall in frustration. He turned on Cerdae. "What about the bodies?"

"We haven't heard anything one way or another," Dykes interjected. "But I'm sure you know the possible implications if the authorities manage to run autopsies."

"Yes, of course I know! So does Tosca! I can't believe that idiot didn't handle any of this himself."

"That's what concerns us," Dykes said. "While all this was going on, apparently he was more concerned about chasing down some runaway so he could have an excuse to drop by and have a little playtime with one of our girls. Does that make any sense to you?"

"Knowing Tosca, yeah, it makes sense, all right," Jeffler said bitterly. "Asshole's brains are between his legs, what do you expect?"

They waited for the elevator, then got on together. Dykes pressed for the ground floor. As they began to descend, the doctor told Jeffler, "I had a strange conversation with Tosca before he left here. He was apparently concerned with what we were doing with the bodies of patients we lost. He said if we were burying them on the property we ought to reconsider. My question is this—do you think he's trying to set us up for blackmail?"

Jeffler thought about it a moment and shook his head. "No, I think you're overestimating him. He was probably just out trying to hustle a few extra bucks."

"But how? Why would he take on the risk of getting rid of bodies when he had no part in their demise?"

"And how do you think he plans on doing it?" Cerdae asked.

The elevator reached the ground floor and the doors hissed open. As he stepped out, Jeffler said, "Quicklime."

"I beg your pardon?" Dykes asked.

"We have vats of it at Sanicorp. Toss a body in there and you aren't going to have to worry about it being discovered."

"And do you think that's what he planned to do with the Simmons family once he had them out of the graves?"

"It'd have to be either that or the incinerators," Jeffler said, gesturing at a phone on the wall. "Let me make a quick call and I can probably find out for sure."

"By all means," Dykes told him.

The deputy picked up the phone and dialed Sanicorp's main office. It took a bit of fast-talking to get the call transferred to the back warehouse without drawing the secretary's suspicions, but finally Jeffler was patched through. He recognized the person answering as Willie Grubb, one of Scotty Sear's closest lieutenants.

"Listen, Willie, I don't have time for bullshit," Jeffler said. "Did you take one of the trucks out to Farthing Meadows today?"

There was a pause on the other end, and when Willie spoke, his voice was lowered to a cautious whisper. "Yeah, and I've been waiting nearly two hours for Scotty to get back with the lab shit."

"You have the bodies with you, don't you." It was a statement, not a question.

"Yeah. And as soon as Scotty gets here we'll—"

"Forget about Scotty!" Jeffler snapped. "Get rid of the bodies. Now!"

"But—"

"Now, Willie! Get them in the quicklime! Do you understand me?"

"Yeah, sure, but there's a lot of people around and I don't know if—"

"If you have to, use the incinerators!" Jeffler barked. "Whatever it takes, just do it! I'm on my way."

Jeffler hung up the phone and glanced at Dykes and Cerdae. "I take it you heard."

"Yes," Dykes said. "We heard."

"Well, then, if you'll excuse me . . ."

The deputy started to leave, but Cerdae side-stepped, blocking his way. "Not so fast."

"What?"

"The contraband you smuggled out of Gerley," Dykes said. "Was there anything else besides what you brought to me?"

"I don't follow."

"Of course you do," Dykes said. "There was a second canister. One of my guards saw you hand it over to Mr. Tosca in the parking lot. Does that help jog your memory?"

Jeffler felt a sick feeling in his stomach. He'd been caught red-handed, and although in his mind he was guilty of nothing other than withholding information, that transgression alone could wind up costing him his life unless he did some fast thinking.

And some fast talking.

"It's Tosca's idea. He figured that as long as he was smuggling stuff for you out of Gerley, he might as well get a few other things he could peddle elsewhere. You know, kill two birds with one stone."

Dykes nodded. "Go on."

"Well, at the same time he's been getting you stuff for your mind-control experiments, he's also been taking some stuff to barter with instead of cash on some coke deals."

"I see," Dykes said. "And these coke deals. Is he doing these through the Bariggia Family?"

Jeffler shook his head. "No, he's dealing straight with the Bolivians."

"And are the Bariggias aware of this?" Cerdae asked.

"Not that I know of. But, listen, I don't have a hell of a lot to do with that. I just get him the stuff from Gerley. What he does with it after he gets it, that's none of my business."

"Of course it isn't," Dykes said with a smile, trading glances with Cerdae. "It's *our* business."

14

Although the vast majority of toxic waste handled by Sanicorp wound up being dumped in isolated areas like the field near the Simmons farm, it would have been a mistake to assume that the company merely ran its operations out of a post-office box. Due to various factors, not the least of which was the need to deal with regulatory aspects of the disposal industry, a token amount of waste picked up by Sanicorp's small fleet of trucks was delivered to the company's Macomb County plant. There, the wastes would be either burned off in high-tech incinerators or transferred into larger holding tanks that, when filled, would be hauled to authorized dump sites. This activity, however small in proportion to the illegal dumping, was adequate enough to keep up appearances, satisfy periodic inspections by outside monitoring teams and provide a backdrop for guided tours for prospective new clients.

The Sanicorp facility was located in an industrial park down the road from Mofo's, sandwiched between a storage complex and a glass-making factory. Both of the latter enterprises, like Sanicorp itself, were

Mob-owned and largely Mob-operated. Members of the Renegades pulled down jobs periodically at all three buildings, not only as a means of claiming legitimate sources of income, but also because each of the businesses fed into the bikers' more lawless activities. The storage facility, for instance, provided an ideal place to keep stolen property as well as drugs. And Tiger Glassworks provided them with bongs and water pipes that could be subsequently peddled at head shops, but also beakers and tubes for use in their clandestine drug labs. The latter materials were usually siphoned off from shipments earmarked for delivery to Gerley Chemical, one of Tiger's biggest clients.

Willie Grubb, right-hand man to Scotty Sear, was the Renegades' primary liaison at the industrial park. He spent time at all three facilities, greasing the necessary palms to keep his fellow bikers tapped into everyday operations and, by the same token, keeping the Renegades on the workforce in line so as not to alienate the other laborers. Grubb enjoyed straddling the two worlds, and he'd done his job so well that he was in the process of being recruited by one of the autoworker's unions to have the Renegades placed "on retainer" in the event their services might be needed to deter scabs from crossing picket lines during an upcoming labor strike. Negotiations were going well, and Grubb felt certain that soon he'd have the deal he was looking for, a deal that would catapult him into the greener pastures of the union hierarchy.

Until he'd gotten the call from Deputy Jeffler. Now he felt that his plans were in severe jeopardy. Obviously something had gone wrong at the cemetery after he'd left with the bodies, and if he was to find himself linked somehow to the grave robbing, he knew he could kiss his aspirations goodbye.

"I'm going on break," he told one of the other workers as he jammed his time card into the time clock in the warehouse employees' lounge.

The truck used in the grave robbery was parked behind the warehouse. Grubb had the keys, but he'd also taken the added precaution of tampering with the engine's wiring to make sure no one else would inadvertently ride off with the bodies. Once he'd hooked things back up, he got behind the wheel and pulled away from the building.

His plan was to drive back to the incinerators, two massive steel cones whose bellies generated enough heat to effectively destroy the toxic agents of certain toxic wastes. He had a good rapport with the furnace operators at one of the burners and knew he'd be able to dismiss the workers from the area long enough to get rid of the bodies without drawing suspicion. But there was a chance that the security cameras focused on the furnace doors around the clock would detect the bodies as they were dumped into the fire. If Jeffler's alarm was founded, however, it was a risk well worth taking, and Grubb figured he could at least partially obscure the camera's view by tossing in a steaming agent prior to dumping the bodies.

As he started for the incinerators, however, Grubb abruptly changed his course and headed for the last in a row of four corrugated steel storage sheds flanking the wall that separated Sanicorp from Tiger Glassworks. A crew of workers was filing out of the shed, and Grubb slowed his truck to avoid encountering them, as they were one of the few groups at Sanicorp that couldn't be counted on to look the other way when other than official business was being conducted. Since the quicklime vats were located in the last shed, Grubb had been wary of trying to destroy the bodies there. Now that the men were leaving, though, it was another matter entirely.

As soon as he saw the men head into the main warehouse, Grubb circled around the far shed, parking next to the back entrance. He got out of the truck and unlocked both the rear doors of the vehicle and the shed's garage door.

The inside of the shed was lined with shelving units stacked high with supplies used in treating all non-drinking water used in the plant's operations. There were replacement parts for various pieces of equipment, sacks of diatomaceous earth and other filtering agents, and, off in the far corner, two huge vats filled with powdered calcium oxide. Quicklime. The substance, created by roasting limestone until all the carbon dioxide had been driven out, was made next door for use in glassmaking, but Sanicorp kept a steady supply as a key ingredient in its water-treatment operations.

And, of course, its highly corrosive properties made it well suited for other needs, as well. A body placed in contact with quicklime would be unrecognizable in minutes, all but obliterated within an hour.

Securing a power forklift, Grubb drove up to the back of the truck, carefully easing the lift's twin prongs into a wooden skid holding three tightly sealed Sanicorp waste drums. The bodies had been stuffed into the drums back at the cemetery, and the seals had been resecured as a defense against the foul smell of decomposing flesh. The drums' lids were fitted with two-inch hose connections, and there were matching hoses mounted to the underside of the quicklime vats. Grubb's plan was not to dump the bodies into the vats, but to link up the hoses and pump each drum full so that the quicklime could do its work without having exposed the bodies and their telltale smell to the open air.

As he lowered his cargo and wheeled the forklift back across the concrete floor of the shed, Willie Grubb felt his fleeting worries beginning to fade. Soon there would be no trace of the Simmons family left to foul his plans.

"Soup's on," he sniggered to himself.

As THE HELICOPTER set down at the far edge of the industrial park, Sheriff Hough quickly briefed Bolan on the layout of the buildings.

"...and Sanicorp's located right next door to Tiger Glassworks. They share a common wall and the same security force, so you might want to keep that in mind."

"Will do," Bolan said. "And you guys?"

Grimaldi said from the pilot's seat, "We'll fly wide and keep an eye on you until you've made penetration, then we'll swoop in and provide a little distraction. The rest is up to you."

Bolan nodded, then swung the copter door open and climbed to the ground, hunching over as he moved beyond range of the overhead rotor. Grimaldi took the aircraft back into the air and banked over the roof of a manufacturing plant that had provided them with cover.

Not wishing to draw undue attention, Bolan kept his Beretta concealed as he rounded the periphery of the industrial park. The park butted up against a wide stream that eventually linked up with the Long Noise River, and there was only a narrow strip of land between the outer wall and a deep slope running to the water's edge. There was litter everywhere, and Bolan's progress was impeded by the constant need to sidestep bits of refuse.

At one point the Executioner drew his gun on a transient who popped unexpectedly into view from behind a discarded deep freezer that had been converted into a makeshift lean-to.

"Whoa, whoa, don't shoot," the drifter said, putting his hands up. "I don't even have a wallet."

"I'm not after you," the Executioner advised, lowering his gun and quickly flashing his Belasko ID.

"I'm a federal agent. Just stay put and out of my way, all right?"

The transient nodded knowingly. "Going to bust somebody, huh? Well, you better watch out for the guards."

"So I've been told," Bolan said as he started to move on, trying to leave the other man behind. The transient dogged his steps, however, expertly weaving his way through the weeds and trash.

"I know this turf like the back of my hand," the man boasted. "You want to sneak up on somebody? I can help."

Bolan glanced up and saw Grimaldi flying wide of the industrial park and close enough to the nearby interstate that the Bell could conceiveably pass for a traffic copter. The ruse could only be maintained for so long before it would be obvious to any guilty parties at Sanicorp that something was amiss. Bolan started to break into a jog to get away from the transient, but at the last second he decided to go with his instincts and see if the man might indeed know the terrain well enough to help save him some time.

"Sanicorp. I need to get on their property without alerting the guards."

"Sanicorp, huh?" The transient frowned and scratched his chin with one hand as he frisked his pockets with the other, coming up with a battered watch. The crystal was cracked and half the wristband was missing, but it still kept time. "You're in luck."

"How's that?" Bolan said warily.

"Follow me." The transient headed off in long strides, crouched over and favoring one leg. Bolan easily kept up with him.

"There's a catering truck that makes the rounds here every day," the transient explained. "Right now it'll be parked out in front of Sanicorp, and the guards always take a breather to grab something to eat. Doughnuts usually."

"How do you know all this?" Bolan asked, wondering vaguely if he might be letting himself be led into a trap.

"Got a lot of time on my hands, that's all." Pointing to a lone pine tree growing at the edge of the nearby stream, he added, "I like to climb up there and keep an eye on things, see how everything works. Ah, here we are...."

They'd reached a length of wall with the Sanicorp logo painted over the brickwork. The wall was nearly ten feet high and topped with baling wire. Scaling it would be difficult, not to mention time-consuming. The transient noticed Bolan's concern.

"You don't have to go that way."

"What do you mean?"

"There's an easier way," the transient said, moving away from the wall and pointing downhill. Bolan glanced down and saw an open-ended concrete pipe poking out of the embankment.

"At night there's usually a lot of water and stuff pouring out, but it should be fairly dry now. It's a tight fit, but you'll be able to get through."

Bolan thanked the man and scrambled down the embankment. He could barely see the men in the helicopter, but he knew that Hough was watching through binoculars, so he gestured that he was going to try to make his way in through the pipe, then turned his attention to the task at hand.

The pipe was six feet in diameter, but there had been rocks cemented into place along the bottom curvature to discourage casual entry, and a little more than ten yards in Bolan encountered a wrought-iron grille. At first look it appeared to be securely anchored in place, effectively blocking his way.

"Don't worry about that," the transient called out behind Bolan. "It's all eaten away by whatever it is they dump through this."

The Executioner glanced back and saw the other man silhouetted in the mouth of the pipe. "Look, I appreciate the help, but I better take it from here on my own."

"Yeah, sure," the man said, disappointment in his voice. "No problem."

Bolan turned back to the grillwork. As the man had said, the mounts had been eaten away and the grille wasn't anchored in place so much as propped against some of the taller rocks. The warrior easily moved it to one side and eased past. As he advanced farther into the darkening shaft, he became increasingly concerned about the trace amounts of liquid under his feet. There was a strong chemical smell in the tunnel, and Bolan was certain that the night dumpings the transient spoke of were probably illegal, and were probably highly volatile, not to mention toxic. He could smell it, and if the stuff was strong enough to eat through wrought iron, he wondered, how long would it take to ravage the soles of his shoes.

Fortunately he didn't have far to go before he came to a junction where the pipe connected with three other shafts, including one that went straight up. By now Bolan was sure he was underneath Sanicorp's grounds, and he started up the perpendicular shaft, taking advantage of ladder rungs set into the concrete. There was just enough light for him to make out a trapdoor overhead. He paused when he reached it, taking out his Beretta and releasing the safety.

He gently pressed upward against the door, and it gave way. Opening it farther, the warrior poked his head up and saw that he was behind one of the incinerators, which effectively shielded him from view of anyone on the grounds.

Once he'd climbed out and reclosed the trapdoor, Bolan catfooted across the asphalt, feeling the heat emanating from the huge furnaces. A hundred yards away, the Bell helicopter was setting down on a section of parking lot, drawing the attention of guards in two different three-wheeled security carts. Several workers were venturing over to the aircraft, too. Bolan and the others had calculated that no one at Sanicorp was going to be as trigger-happy as the bikers at the Renegades' compound and thusfar they were right. To be on the safe side, however, Bolan kept his Beretta clenched in his right hand.

There was a lot of ground to be covered, but the Executioner confined himself primarily with tracking down any small trucks that might have been used in the body heists at the cemetery. As he made his way behind the row of sheds lying in the shadow of Tiger Glassworks, he spotted one such truck and cautiously approached it.

The back doors of the vehicle were open, and when Bolan peered inside, he could see that whatever cargo it had been carrying had already been unloaded. He was about to turn around to investigate the shed behind him when he detected a blur of motion out of the corner of his eye.

Instinctively the warrior leaned away, but even his reflexes weren't quick enough to keep a three-foot length of two-by-four lumber from crashing against his head. He reeled to the ground and didn't get up.

Willie Grubb stared down at his victim, then glanced around to make sure no one had witnessed the attack. Satisfied, he pulled Bolan into the shed and dragged him toward the quicklime.

"Maybe I'm going to have to throw somebody in after all."

15

Bolan was unconscious for only a few moments.

When he came to, though, he remained motionless on the cold concrete floor, trying to regain his bearings. He was on his back, and he could feel a throbbing in his shoulders and at the base of his skull from where he'd been struck. He assumed that whoever had knocked him out had also relieved him of his Beretta, leaving him at an even further disadvantage.

He could hear someone moving about inside the shed, and the noise seemed to be coming from overhead. Knowing that he might betray himself by looking up, he nonetheless slowly opened his eyes just enough to be able to peer through his lashes.

The first thing that fell within the warrior's field of vision was the fifty-gallon drum he was lying next to. He saw that there was a hose linking the drum to a nearby raised stainless-steel tank. A man was standing on a platform, unfastening clamps that secured the tank's lid. The handle of Bolan's automatic was visible above the waistline of the guy's slacks. He glanced back down at Bolan every few seconds, making it difficult for the Executioner to get a clearer idea of what he'd stumbled onto. There was a stenciled label on the side of the tank, however, and from where he was lying Bolan could make out a few of the large letters.

ICKLI.

Quicklime.

He'd encountered the substance enough times in the past to know its deadly potential, and it became suddenly clear what kind of fate his captor had in store for him.

Assessing his situation, Bolan decided his best bet was to stay put and play possum until the guy came down from the platform. Then, when the man tried to drag him up to the vat, Bolan could spring into action.

Fate intervened before the Sanicorp employee could be drawn into Bolan's trap, however. As he was drawing back the lid to the vat, the Renegade heard someone else inside the shed and he whirled around.

The transient, having ignored Bolan's advice, had followed the Executioner to the shed and was now in the process of trying to play hero. Throwing a security switch mounted to the wall, the man triggered an alarm that shrieked loudly both inside and outside the shed.

"Okay, the jig's up!" he called out as he ducked for cover behind the forklift.

"Son of a bitch!" Grubb shouted above the siren. He yanked out Bolan's Beretta and fired at the transient, raising sparks off the surface of the forklift.

Bolan took advantage of the diversion, rolling to his feet. By the time Grubb realized Bolan had come to, the Executioner was already halfway up the steps leading to the platform. Grubb swung the Beretta around, but before he could get off another shot, the warrior lashed out with a karate kick, stabbing the biker's wrist with his toe and dislodging the gun.

As the men struggled on the platform, the transient moved out from behind the forklift and sought out the Beretta where it had fallen on the ground. Picking up the weapon, he raised it into firing position, but Grubb and Bolan were fighting at such close quarters he didn't dare shoot.

Grubb was taller than Bolan, but thinner and more gangly. Like most of the other Renegades, he was no stranger to street fighting, and he didn't waste his effort on Hollywood-style fisticuffs. At the same time he was trying to tie Bolan up with his long, strapping arms, he jabbed hard with his knees and elbows, seeking out his opponent's groin, throat and face, where blows would do the most harm. Bolan, with even more experience at hand-to-hand combat, anticipated such moves, however, and fended most of them off while parrying with his own series of compact martial-arts jabs.

As they slammed into the outer railing of the platform, Bolan finally managed to break free of Grubb's hold. Rather than bounding away, he took advantage of his greater mobility to move in and position himself so he could use his adversary's own height and weight against him. A well-placed elbow to the ribs stunned Grubb long enough for Bolan to twist around and plant his feet, then flip the biker over his shoulder. Grubb let out a scream as he felt himself pulled off his feet and sent flying into the open vat of quicklime. His cry was silenced as he plunged into the crushed powder headfirst.

Bolan rushed to the inner railing and leaned over, trying to grab the man. The way he was flailing, however, Grubb kicked Bolan's hands away and burrowed farther into the lethal quagmire, hastening his own doom. By the time he stopped struggling, the Renegade was almost completely submerged. Bolan knew there was no point in trying to save him.

"That was close," the transient said, raising his voice to be heard above the shrill bleating of the alarm.

"I thought I told you to stay put," Bolan said as he headed down the steps to retrieve his Beretta. Offering a thin smile, he added, "Thanks for not listening."

As the warrior crossed the shed to shut off the alarm, he was intercepted by Grimaldi, Hough and two security guards. One of the guards had a key that fit the siren box, and as soon as he inserted it and gave it a turn, the shed fell silent.

"Everything all right here?" Hough asked he looked around the shed.

"Depends on what side you're on," Bolan said. He went on to quickly describe his encounter with the employee.

"Well, if he had just managed to take the lid off the quicklime, then maybe the bodies are still intact," Grimaldi said hopefully.

"Not necessarily." Bolan led the others to the three fifty-gallon drums and pointed to the hose linking one of them to the tank. "The valve's been opened." He tapped the side of the drum, and from the sound of it they could tell that it had already been filled with quicklime.

"Which means if there's a body in this drum, we aren't going to get a look at it," Grimaldi surmised.

"Afraid so," Bolan said.

Hough moved to the other two drums and tapped them. Both sounded hollower than the other one. "Doesn't sound like he got to these yet, though."

"That can be corrected," one of the guards interrupted, raising his service revolver and aiming it at Hough. "Get away from those drums."

The other guard pulled his gun out as well, waving it back and forth at Grimaldi and Bolan. "And don't make any move for your weapons or you're dead."

As they followed the command, Grimaldi glanced at Hough and said, "I knew they were being a little too cooperative."

"Shut up!" the first guard snapped.

"Oh, big men with their little guns!" the transient taunted, taking a step toward the guards. "I'm not afraid of you."

"The feeling's mutual, punk," the second guard said. He did a sudden double-take and looked harder at the transient. "Hey, don't I know you?"

"Yeah. I used to work here. Remember? Dale James. I was going to blow the whistle on the night dumpings, but you guys and a couple of your buddies dragged me out by the stream and worked me over. Did a good job, too. Left me for dead."

"If you were smart, you would have stayed that way," the second guard told him.

"No, I wanted to wait until I had a chance to pay you back," James said as he took another step toward the guards. "I've been keeping an eye on you. I know even more than I did when I worked here."

"Still don't know enough to keep your mouth shut, though." The first guard casually pointed his revolver at the transient's chest and pulled the trigger. James's eyes widened and he took the hit and staggered backward.

As the man slumped to the ground, Bolan and Grimaldi simultaneously sprang into action. The Executioner drew his Beretta, Grimaldi his Government Model .45. During the ensuing gunfire, Hough yanked out his service revolver and joined in. Shots rang out loudly in the confined space, and it was over almost as quickly as it had started.

The two guards were both slain. Bulletproof vests had spared the others from mortal wounds, but Grimaldi and Hough had taken bullets in the thigh and arm, respectively. Bolan leaned over Dale James, who was still alive but bleeding heavily.

"We'll get you to a hospital," he said.

"Don't know if I'll last that long," James gasped. He forced a grin as he glanced at the gunman who'd shot him. "He nailed me good."

"Look, just stay put and be quiet until we get some help."

The transient shook his head. "Might be better if I give you a statement. Like I was saying, I got the goods on these guys. I'll die in peace knowing I was able to stick it back to them."

"I'll stay with him," Grimaldi offered, grimacing as he tied a handkerchief around his thigh. "I've got a through-and-through, so I'll be okay. Go get us an ambulance."

As Bolan and Hough departed the shed, the sheriff rolled up his sleeve to inspect where he'd been shot. "Hell, mine's just a scratch, too."

"I'm glad," Bolan said. "Now if we can just—"

He fell silent. Up ahead, somebody was climbing down from another Sanicorp truck that had pulled up to the shed. It was Todd Jeffler.

"Well, well, you're sure a sight for sore eyes," Hough called out, startling his deputy.

When Jeffler spotted Bolan and Hough, his hand went for his gun.

"Don't try it," Hough warned, hauling out his service revolver.

Jeffler drew his gun anyway. Before he could fire, though, Hough drilled him with a chest shot. Bewildered, the deputy stumbled backward, leaning against the front of his truck. He dropped his gun and stared at Hough a moment, then his legs gave out and he sprawled to the asphalt.

The sheriff shook his head, ashen-faced, and slowly holstered his gun. "Okay," he told Bolan. "That leaves Rosey Tosca."

THE MURRY ATHLETIC CLUB dated back to the days when boxing at the Olympic was in its prime and contenders from all weight divisions spent endless hours in the old brownstone's gymnasium, training for the next big fight or recuperating from the last one. Times had changed, however. A few die-hard boxers still worked out in the gym, but membership fees had skyrocketed since a recent change in ownership and a multimillion-dollar renovation transformed the club from a lower-class sweat hole into an upscale fitness emporium whose clientele consisted primarily of white-collar executives battling the tireless war against middle-age paunch.

Rosey Tosca had joined the facility after its most recent incarnation, finding it, like the track at Hazel Park, an ideal place to court and build a network of new clients. It was at Murry's, for instance, that Tosca had made his acquaintance with many of his cocaine clients, and it was also where he'd first met Frankie Cerdae and Dr. Mark Dykes. Considering that the club's new owner was a nephew of Jimmy Bariggia, it was no surprise that it was also here that Tosca had solidified his ties to the Mob.

Now, sitting in the sauna after swimming forty laps in the club's Olympic-size pool, Tosca was debating whether to cut the Bariggias in on tonight's drug deal. There were obvious advantages. The Bariggias were longtime pros at handling the Detroit drug trade, and a little added backup might come in handy when he went face-to-face with the Bolivians in Wyandotte. Of course, there might be some hard feelings when it became clear that Tosca would have handled the deal on his own under other circumstances and was only bringing them in at the last minute. The implication, of course, was that Tosca had, at least at one point, entertained plans of cutting into the Bariggia's stranglehold on the upper rungs of the Michigan coke market. The fact that Tosca was dealing with Bolivians rather than the Medellín connections favored by the Mob was also something that wouldn't sit well with Jimmy Bariggia. Many men had died for launching far less ambitious schemes, some of them slain by Tosca's own hand.

As he got out of the sauna and padded his way down the corridor to the masseuse's room, Tosca's attention was drawn to a television mounted from the ceiling near the juice bar. The news was on, and when the headline stories were announced, it was all the hardman could do to maintain his composure.

The lead story, not surprisingly, dealt with the shoot-out at the cemetery and the disappearance of the bodies of the Simmons family. The Renegades had been implicated in both the gunfire and the grave robbing, and connections were being made to the earlier attempt on the life of Helena Simmons and a federal agent.

That news, in and of itself, was disturbing enough to Tosca. But then the station switched to a live report from Sanicorp's Macomb County disposal plant, where a reporter divulged that there had been yet another shoot-out on the facility grounds, in the aftermath of which all but two of the missing bodies had been found stuffed into Sanicorp waste drums. Already the press was speculating that illegal waste dumping might have had something to do with the as-yet unsolved Simmons murders. It was reported that one of the suspects in the killings had been gunned down during the Sanicorp shoot-out, and another suspect was now the subject of a city-wide manhunt.

Tosca braced himself and fought back a wave of panic, fearing that any second he was going to see his likeness flashed across the television screen. Fortunately for him, though, the reporter apparently hadn't been given any names. Coverage switched back to the newsroom and the anchorperson moved on the to next story, which concerned the aftermath of Hell Night.

The hardman turned and walked past the massage room, sticking his head in just long enough to cancel his scheduled massage. Given the circumstances, Tosca knew that he was beyond any hope of relaxing, and he wanted to get dressed as soon as possible, fearing that at any moment the authorities might somehow trace him to the club.

After a quick shower, Tosca changed his clothes and headed for the main desk. As he was waiting in line to turn in his locker key, he saw a uniformed police officer emerge from the membership office, talking with none other than Jimmy Bariggia's nephew, Augusto Murry. Tosca couldn't hear what was being said, but to be on the safe side, he turned his back to the two men and discreetly unzipped his gym bag, providing himself with easy access to his .357 Magnum nestled in the folds of his sweats.

As Murry and the cop ventured closer, Tosca slowly reached inside the bag, closing his fingers around the gun. If worse came to worst, he figured he could grab somebody in the line and hold him hostage while he bartered for his freedom.

It turned out, however, that his paranoia, at least at this point, was unfounded. As the men walked past him, Tosca overheard enough snatches of their conversation to realize that the cop was merely following up on the reported theft of a stereo system from a Porsche owned by one of the club's members.

"Yeah, we're going to have to beef up our parking-lot security," Murry told the cop as he led him to the main entrance.

"Might be a real good idea. You keep having break-ins this often, you're going to start losing members."

"I hear you," Murry said. "Thanks for the tip."

After letting the cop out, Murry remained near the doorway, talking with a couple other members. Tosca didn't want to risk getting bogged down in a conversation with the man at this point. Maybe later, if and when the heat died down. For now, Tosca's instincts were geared more toward survival.

Once he got his membership card back, Tosca detoured to a bank of pay phones, where he could see Murry's reflection in a nearby glass door. As he waited for the owner to leave the entranceway, the hardman made a call to Zane Ackson, his next-door neighbor in Ridon and a trusted friend. Ackson had no idea what kind of activities Tosca was involved with, but he assumed it was nothing more than some kind of gray-area entrepreneurship. Tosca had planted the idea in Ackson's head on countless occasions, referring to himself as a modern-day Robin Hood committed to robbing from the rich to give to the poor. Tosca knew he could count on the man's discretion.

"Zane, buddy," Tosca said when the man answered the phone.

"Hey, Rosey! Am I glad to hear your voice!"

"Why? What's wrong?"

"I don't know, but I thought you could tell me."

"I'm not sure what you're getting at, Zane."

"Well, your dogs have been going nuts all afternoon," Ackson told him, "and whenever I take a peek out through the blinds, I keep seeing strange cars driving by. Smells like some kind of undercover operation...like they're waiting to spring a trap on you."

"Well, I sure appreciate you tipping me off, Zane," Tosca told him. "And you pretty much figured it out, only they aren't undercover cops."

"No?"

"No, they're security people for Motown City Savings and Loan."

"Huh?"

"You know, the ones involved in that big scandal," Tosca said, making up his cover story as he went along. "They took all this money from poor Joes like you and me, then lost it all on junk bonds and stuff."

"Yeah, I heard all about them," Ackson said. "Bastards."

"Exactly, which is why they're out to get me," Tosca lied. "You see, a friend and I, we found a way to tap into their computers, and we managed to track down some money and get it transferred into our hands so we can help pay off some of the people who've lost their life savings."

"Yeah?"

"Yeah," Tosca said, "but it's going to take awhile longer for us to pull it all off, so in the meantime I'm counting on you, Zane. Can you keep an eye on my place? I'll check in to see when they've let up on their surveillance."

"Anything I can do," Ackson said. "You can count on me."

"I know that," Tosca said. "You're like my Friar Tuck."

"Yeah!"

In the glass, Tosca saw Murry finally leaving the main entrance. "Okay, I got to go, Zane. I'll be in touch, though."

Tosca got off the phone and quickly exited the club. He drove his car three blocks, then pulled down a side alley and parked. Using his cellular phone, he patched through a call to his home phone. He'd been careful to keep no evidence of his criminal activities in the house, but in the event the authorities might break in and search the place, there was still one Achilles' heel that could potentially incriminate him. When his answering machine clicked on, he entered the appropriate code and screened the messages. As he'd suspected, there was a call from Jax Allmus, his contact with the Bolivians, regarding the cocaine transaction slated for tonight. Apparently something had gone awry and Tosca was supposed to call to make new arrangements. The message was coded, but Tosca was wary that if the right people intercepted the message they'd be able to crack the code and figure out what was going down.

Using remote signals, Tosca erased the messages and shut down the answering machine so it wouldn't take any future calls. Then he put a quick call through to Allmus. The news wasn't as bad as he'd feared. Apparently a warehouse next door to where Tosca was supposed to make the deal in Wyandotte had been burned down during the Hell Night arson spree. It was feared that between the presence of police and the media, it'd be too risky to have the transaction take place there.

"No problem," Tosca said. "I can think of a few other places we can do it."

"We have a place in mind already," Allmus told him. "A miniature golf park owned by one of our people. Let me give you directions."

As Tosca jotted down the information, he realized the park ironically was only about five miles from the Beta Institute. If he had gotten in touch with Allmus a few hours earlier, he could have saved himself a lot of driving. No matter. Compared to everything else that had gone wrong today, it seemed a minor inconvenience.

"I can be there in about two hours," Tosca said, glancing at his watch.

"Fine. We'll be expecting you."

Tosca hung up and drove out of the alley, turning on the radio and switching to a classical music station to distract himself. He'd be glad when this whole episode was over, and when it was, he was toying with the idea of taking some time off. The Caribbean sounded inviting. Rent a place on the beach and spend a week sipping piña coladas, listening to the surf and getting laid by high-priced hookers. Let this whole mess in Motown blow over, then come back and reposition himself.

His pleasant reverie lasted only until the end of the Beethoven sonata playing on the radio. When the station broke away for news and he heard yet another report on the grave robbing and the shoot-out at Sanicorp, his paranoia kicked back into high gear.

He was two blocks from the interstate he'd planned on taking to his rendezvous, but suddenly detoured, taking side streets until he pulled into one of the largest shopping malls in Detroit. He parked his car in a relatively conspicuous place, then got out with his gym bag and opened the trunk, removing a larger satchel containing the canister with the stolen vials from Gerley Chemical. He carried the items to the nearest corner and flagged down a taxi. He figured if the police had an APB out for his car and they found it at the mall, they'd waste time and manpower searching the stores for him. In the meantime, he'd be on the other side of town, handling the coke transaction.

"Where to?" the cabbie asked as Tosca got into the back of the taxi.

Tosca gave directions, then sat back in the seat and let out a long sigh.

"Miniature golf, huh?" the cabbie said as he drove off. "Man, I hate those things. Too many obstacles always getting in your way."

"Yeah, but if you get past the obstacles and score a hole in one, it's great."

16

After the dust had settled at Sanicorp, ambulances had taken the wounded to a nearby hospital. Sheriff Hough's arm wound, it turned out, had been more serious than at first thought, and he was recuperating in post-op after having had microsurgery to correct some muscle and nerve damage left by the bullet. Grimaldi had fared better, being given an okay to leave after being treated, although he was under doctor's orders to use crutches to keep weight off his injured thigh while it healed. The entire leg was stiff and throbbing with pain, but it didn't interfere with his ability to operate the Bell helicopter. He was at the controls now, bound for Helena Simmons's Talville Terrace apartment with Bolan to search through her magazine notes for any possible clues that might shed light on Sanicorp's contact at Gerley Chemical.

Bolan was in radio communication with Brognola at Mosenan Isle, bringing the man up-to-date. Once he'd finished, the warrior asked, "How's Helena?"

"She's going to be fine. In fact, she's been up most of the day, putting together a list of all the files you might want to call up on her computer."

"She knows that off the top of her head?"

"Not only that," Brognola replied, "but she also knows which back issues of the magazine contain stories that might be relevant to what we're looking for. I'm faxing the list to the apartment manager, and he'll hand it over to the guys doing surveillance on the apartment so they can give it to you."

"She doesn't miss a beat, does she?" Bolan remarked.

"Not if she can help it."

"I take it no one's tried to get to her at the infirmary."

"Affirmative. But if they should, I'm sure Able Team will take care of matters."

"I'm sure they will, too."

"I heard back from Bear," the big Fed said, abruptly changing the subject. "He's come up with some intriguing info on that old Farthing Meadows asylum. I'm not sure how, but I think it ties in with what's happening now."

"Yeah?"

"It seems that back in the late fifties and early sixties," Brognola explained, "the CIA had some of its scientists on staff at Farthing."

"CIA?" Bolan said.

"That's right. Apparently they were conducting mind-control experiments on patients."

"I know some of that went on out on the West Coast," Bolan said, "but not here."

"Well, Bear's got documentation. And here's where it gets interesting. The tests were done using hallucinogens and other drugs provided by none other than—"

"Gerley Chemical," Bolan interjected.

"Interesting, eh?"

"Sure as hell is."

"I had Bear fax me a list of the various drugs they were working with back then," Brognola said. "Guess what?"

"They're some of the same drugs being smuggled out of Gerley."

"Exactly. I've spent the past hour charting all the missing inventory, and it seems like it breaks down into three groups. Of course, we already know about all the things pertaining to chemical and biological warfare, and there's a second group of supplies that can be linked to the Renegades and their drug labs. You take away that stuff and what you're left with is a list that nearly matches up, item by item, with what CIA was using at Farthing. The only exceptions are that in some cases newer generations of drugs have replaced things being used back then."

"So are you saying that the Company's behind the thefts?"

"No, I don't think so," Brognola said, quickly adding, "at least not in any official capacity."

"Meaning..."

"Meaning, in 1962 word got out that patients were being used as guinea pigs, and CIA bailed out of

Farthing Meadows. A lot of families filed lawsuits against the asylum, which is why the place finally shut down. The man heading up the CIA team was a psychotherapist named Frederick Sigfreid. He got the boot and left the country. That was in 1963. He hasn't been heard from since."

"And you think he's resurfaced thirty years later?"

"I'm not sure," Brognola said. "It just all seems a little too coincidental."

"Well, once we find whoever's behind the thefts at Gerley we'll hopefully have some answers," Bolan said. Glancing out the window, he could see they were coming up on Talville Terrace Apartments. "Look, we're about ready to check Helena's place. If we come up with anything, I'll let you know."

The two men signed off. Grimaldi brought the aircraft down in a field adjacent to the apartment complex. The two-man security detail running surveillance on Helena's apartment had been forewarned about their arrival and greeted Bolan and Grimaldi with a master key secured from the manager, along with the fax sheet containing the file information in Helena's computer. Almost as an afterthought, they reported no suspicious activity since they'd started their vigil.

"You can handle the magazines and I'll check the computer," Bolan said as he and Grimaldi entered the apartment. He tore the fax sheet in two, giving Grimaldi the list of which back issues of *Detroit Monthly* bore looking into.

As Grimaldi tackled the magazines, Bolan tracked down Helena's computer in the den and turned it on. Referring to the list of files, he called them up one by one, skimming the notes for relevant information.

"Here's something interesting," Grimaldi called out from across the room. "In this article about bike gangs, she claims the Renegades muscled out another club in the coke market by cutting a deal with the Bariggia Family."

"That pretty much fits in with what we've seen," Bolan said. "It makes sense too, if you figure Hough said Bariggia's got his meat hooks in nearly every kind of action around town."

"Including Gerley Chemical, I'll bet." Grimaldi flipped a few more pages into the article on bike gangs. "Hey, here's a group shot of the Renegades. And this guy here, he's one of the security guards at Sanicorp we had to take out."

"Yeah?"

"You know," Grimaldi said, "I wonder if maybe we shouldn't get hold of ID photos of workers at Gerley. Maybe we'd get a match with—"

"Won't be necessary," Bolan interrupted, staring at the computer monitor in front of him.

"Why's that?"

"I think I found our turncoat," Bolan explained, waving Grimaldi over. "Take a look at these notes from one of her interviews with employees at Gerley's warehouse."

Grimaldi peered over Bolan's shoulder at the screen. A telltale name jumped out from the list of interviewees.

"Timothy Jeffler."

"Any relation to the deputy?" Grimaldi wondered.

"Maybe we should track him down and ask him," Bolan said, shutting off the computer.

IT WAS DUSK when Rosey Tosca's taxi pulled over to the curb in front of the Hole-in-Fun miniature golf course. The hardman got out, giving the cabbie a modest tip, then lugged his two bags across the parking lot.

The Hole-in-Fun had seen better days. The Astro-turf putting greens were worn through to the concrete in places, and all the fixtures were in dire need of fresh paint. Although the park was open for another hour, there were only three cars in the parking lot, two of them belonging to employees. The lone players were a pair of high-school sweethearts, giddily chasing their balls around a half-size windmill. They were having the time of their lives.

Tosca wandered over to a small building just inside the main gate. There was a burly black man behind the front counter, flipping idly through a newspaper.

"Nine or eighteen holes," he asked.

"I'm supposed to meet someone."

The other man gave the new arrival a quick once-over, then said, "Not here yet."

"He's never late," Tosca said, checking his clock. "He should have been here already."

"Hey, what can I say?" The other man shrugged, gesturing lazily to a nearby door. "He said you could wait inside."

"That's okay." Tosca took a step back, suddenly on his guard. He was further startled when he felt something hard prod him in the small of his back.

"It's warmer inside," the man behind him whispered. "And, here, let me help you with your bags."

Tosca knew he'd wandered into a trap, and he also knew the only way he was going to get out of it alive was to act fast and think even faster.

"Hey, if I wanted a porter, I would have gone to a hotel." Tosca laughed, trying to buy some time. He glanced over his shoulder, catching a quick glimpse of his captor, who was a head shorter and a good fifty pounds lighter. Tosca didn't recognize him but suspected he, like his contact and the man inside the shop, was Bolivian.

"You'll wait inside," the short man suggested again. "And I'll take your bags."

"Fine, but don't expect a big tip," Tosca said with a shrug. He was glad he'd transferred his .357 Magnum from his gym bag to his coat while he was in the taxi, but he still needed to get to it without having his spine blown away by the short Bolivian.

Out of the corner of his eye Tosca could see the short man reaching for the larger bag. When the man's fingers were just starting to close around the handle,

Tosca let go of the bag. The Bolivian reflexively lunged forward, grasping for a better hold. In doing so, he momentarily pulled his gun away from Tosca's back. It was all the time the hardman needed.

Jerking his arm back as hard and as fast as he could, Tosca rammed his elbow into his adversary's face, dislocating his jaw and sending him reeling off balance into a rack of putters. His gun went off accidentally, burying lead in the asphalt at Tosca's feet.

Tosca whipped out his pistol and planted two .357 slugs in the short man's chest, then quickly spun to face the other Bolivian, who was reaching for something beneath the counter.

"Drop it or you're dead!" Tosca warned.

Out on the miniature course the teenage girl screamed. Her boyfriend grabbed her by the arms and dragged her behind the cover of a shoulder-high plaster stegosaurus lording over the seventh hole.

The Bolivian warily pulled his hands away from the counter. There was fear in his eyes as he stared at Tosca. "I don't know anything!" he pleaded. "Allmus just told me to have you wait inside. I swear, it's all I know."

Tosca leaned across the counter, keeping the gun trained on the other man. He reached down and came up with a .22-caliber carbine, aiming it at the man as well.

"Where's Allmus?"

"He's on his way," the Bolivian replied. He gestured at the corpse, which lay in a sprawl near the putters. "Don was supposed to make sure you brought the stuff, then keep you prisoner until he arrived."

"Well, there's been a change of plans," Tosca said. "Put your keys on the counter and tell me which car is yours."

The Bolivian carefully reached into his pockets and took out a ringful of keys, separating one before setting them on the counter. "Mine's the Taurus."

Tosca grabbed the keys, then calmly pulled the trigger on the carbine. The Bolivian had no chance to react before .22-caliber slugs ripped through his throat and upper chest. Like his comrade, he died instantly, toppling over a folding chair set next to the register.

Tucking the carbine under his arm, Tosca picked up the large bag containing the contraband he'd planned to trade to Allmus for cocaine. Taking long strides across the parking lot, he glanced out at the golf course, which stood out in silhouette against a breathtaking orange-and-purple sunset. There was no trace of the high-schoolers, and Tosca wasn't about to waste time hunting them down.

Halfway to the Taurus, he spotted a white limousine speeding down the road toward the park. He knew it had to be Allmus, and he also knew he didn't have time to get to the Ford and make a getaway.

"Shit," he spit, detouring to his left and charging onto the golf course.

The limousine veered into the parking lot and screeched to a halt. The front doors swung open and two Bolivians scrambled out, both of them armed with

.38 automatics. They directed their fire at Tosca as he fled into the maze of obstacles. A scaled-down replica of a space shuttle took a couple hits and shattered.

The hardman made his first stand behind the cover of a small concrete bridge. He emptied the carbine at the two other gunners, killing one and pinning the other near the entrance to the course. In the background, he saw the rear door open on the far side of the limo. He couldn't see who got out, but assumed it was Allmus. He didn't want to waste precious ammo taking long-distance potshots, though.

Breaking from cover, he dodged more gunfire and leaped over an oversize plaster turtle. As he approached the windmill, he spotted the trembling high-school couple and moved beside them.

"You," he told the boy. "On a count of three, make a run for it."

"But they'll think I'm you," the youth protested.

"Don't argue," Tosca said. He grabbed the girl and pressed the barrel of his pistol against her temple. "One...two..."

Tears in his eyes, the boy swallowed hard and bolted from the cover of the windmill. He only got a few yards before being mowed down.

"You bastard!"

"Shut up!" Tosca gritted in the girl's ear. "Shut up or you're next!"

Tosca debated trying to use the girl as a hostage or human shield, but he knew it wouldn't work. Not with

Allmus. The Bolivian would have no qualms about seeing the girl dead if that was what it would take.

Before he could take another course of action, Tosca was distracted by the loud thump of something bouncing off the side of the windmill. He saw a roundish object fall to the putting green and roll toward the cup.

Grenade.

Acting on instinct, Tosca shoved the girl toward the projectile. It went off before she could land on it. Had it been a fragmentary grenade, she, and no doubt Tosca as well, would have been brutally rent limb from limb and buried in rubble. But what Allmus had hurled was a Morlick BL-10, a high-tech flash-and-stun grenade designed specifically to disable foes without dismembering them and to minimize collateral damage. The weapon worked well enough, giving off a blinding flash of light and concussive shock waves that reversed the girl's headlong fall and blew her backward. Tosca was hurled off his feet and slammed into the windmill with enough force to knock the wind from his lungs. The concurrent flash of light temporarily blinded him, as well.

As Tosca dropped to his knees, wheezing for breath and groping the ground for his dropped gun, Allmus and the other Bolivian quickly caught up with him. Allmus was brandishing an M-16 rifle, and after stepping over the unconscious girl he lashed out with the rifle's stock, smacking it against the side of Tosca's head. The hardman toppled sideways to the ground, clinging to a faint shred of consciousness. Blood seeped through a gash in his scalp.

"Looks like you hurt your head, Rosey," Allmus murmured as he and the other Bolivian lifted Tosca to his feet. "You're in luck, though. I happen to know a doctor just down the road. Maybe you've heard of him. His name is Dr. Dykes...."

17

Tim Jeffler had been at work when he'd received word of his brother's death during the shoot-out at Sanicorp. His foreman, who'd broken the news, gave Jeffler the rest of the day off.

As he drove away from the Gerley plant, Tim tried to fight off his panic and plot his next move. His boss had given only sketchy details about the circumstances surrounding Todd's death, but after tuning in to the local all-news radio station, Tim heard enough about the raid at Sanicorp to guess that the authorities had established the link between the waste-disposal company and the theft of classified materials from Gerley Chemical. Given that and the fact that Todd had been killed during the raid, it seemed equally likely that the cops would consider Tim a suspect by virtue of the fact that he was Todd's brother. If he was lucky, he figured he was maybe a few steps ahead of the law. His best bet was to keep it that way by making a run for it.

But first he had to make one stop.

Wolverine Savings and Loan had a branch office near the chemical plant that stayed open until seven on

weekdays. Jeffler arrived a few minutes before closing. He had sixteen thousand dollars in a money-
market account. He left a thousand in the account and
withdrew the rest in cash, offering the teller a hastily
concocted story about needing the money to buy a car
from a private party. He also asked for access to his
safe-deposit box. In it were a few classified papers he'd
confiscated from Gerley Chemical in recent weeks. He
wasn't as familiar with the workings of the black
market as his brother, but he knew that the papers
were worth more money than he'd have gotten if he'd
brokered them through Todd.

Once he pulled out of the bank lot, Jeffler directed
his Olds Cutlass down a back road. He was only a few
miles from I-75, and he figured he'd drive the interstate all the way north to the Upper Peninsula. From
there he'd cross over into Wisconsin. He knew that his
boss had an isolated summer cabin near Laona in the
Nicolet National Forest. This time of year the cabin
would be boarded up for the off-season, and there was
no other residence within a seven-mile radius. Tim
could buy a carload of rations, break into the cabin
and hole up for a few weeks. That would give him
plenty of time to sort things out and decide what to do
next.

There was no other traffic on the road, and Jeffler
was startled when he heard what sounded like another vehicle. He turned down his radio and quickly
realized that the sound was coming from overhead.
Glancing out his side window, he could make out the

lights of a helicopter in the night sky. It was flying low and seemed to be matching his speed so that it stayed relatively the same distance from his Olds. When he eased down on the accelerator, the copter picked up speed as well.

"Goddamn," Jeffler cursed, feeling a renewed sense of dread.

He pushed the pedal to the floor, rousing his 2.8-liter engine. The Cutlass plunged forward, its tires squealing as it rounded a turn and bolted down a straight stretch of roadway. The thunder of the car's V6 drowned out the chopper, and Jeffler didn't dare take his eyes off the road. He could see the lights of the interstate a mile away. If he could just get there, he felt certain he could shake the copter in traffic.

As fast as he pushed the Cutlass, however, the Bell was faster. It swooped down into view, passing over the top of the car and racing ahead of it. Jeffler wasn't sure what the pilot was up to, but he continued to speed on.

Once the helicopter had outrun the Olds by a good hundred yards, it slowed and eerily spun around, dropping to within a few feet of the roadway. As Jeffler bore down on it, the chopper suddenly flashed on a high-powered searchlight mounted on its nose.

Jeffler was unprepared for the maneuver. In the process of reflexively throwing up one hand to shield his eyes from the blinding glare, he jerked the steering wheel to one side. At the speed he was going, it was just enough to force the car out of control. Jeffler pulled his foot off the accelerator as he clawed at the wheel, but the Olds had a mind of its own and hurtled off the road.

A few yards beyond the shoulder was a shallow ravine. The Olds sped down the incline at an angle, nearly flipping as it plowed through heaps of fallen leaves and thick mud. The obstacles slowed the car considerably, and by the time it bounded up the other side of the ravine, the speedometer was registering less than twenty miles an hour. That was still enough momentum, however, to total the vehicle as it broadsided one, then another thick oak tree before finally coming to a stop.

Jeffler had been driving with his seat belt on, but the collision had still taken a toll. Dazed and bruised, it took him a few seconds to compose himself. He unclipped the belt and leaned across the front seat, opening the glove compartment. As he was reaching for a handgun, however, the passenger door suddenly swung open. Mack Bolan grabbed Jeffler by the wrist and jerked him halfway out of the car.

"Let's have a talk," the Executioner growled.

BOLAN AND GRIMALDI had been put onto Jeffler's scent thanks to the teller at Wolverine Savings and Loan, who'd added up Jeffler's suspicious bank activity with the fact that his slain brother had just been linked to criminal activity and deduced that Tim had withdrawn most of his funds for something other than a car purchase. She'd voiced her concerns to her boss, who in turn had relayed the information to the FBI. Hal Brognola was on top of all Bureau activity relative to the espionage investigations at Gerley, and when he got the news he'd put through a call to Bolan and Grimaldi, who at the time were en route to Jeffler's home address. Provided with the location of the savings and loan and a description of Jeffler's car, the men had detoured to Talville, spotting the vehicle on the country road.

And now they had him.

An ambulance had been summoned, as had been the FBI, but while they waited to turn Jeffler over, Bolan and Grimaldi wanted some answers. The fact that he'd been found with stolen documents from Gerley negated any chance that he might protest his innocence, but Jeffler steadfastly denied any knowledge of what happened after he handed materials over to his brother or left them at the drop site.

"I think he's stonewalling," Grimaldi told Bolan.

"I am not," Jeffler insisted. "Look, I don't know any more details because I didn't want to get that involved. Why can't you believe me?"

Bolan showed Jeffler the packet of stolen documents. "For starters, if you're in the dark, why were you carrying these around after you already knew your brother was dead? What did you think you were going to do with them?"

"I don't know," Jeffler admitted. "Maybe I wanted a little insurance. Maybe I wanted something in case I ever changed my mind and wanted to... to..."

"In case you ever wanted to betray your country a little more than you already had," Grimaldi snapped, raising one of his crutches and prodding Jeffler with its rubber tip. "You goddamn traitor! I ought to spare everybody a trial and take you out right here, right now."

"Easy," Bolan intervened, swiping the crutch to one side. As planned, he was playing good cop to Grimaldi's bad cop. "Give him a chance to talk."

"Why?" Grimaldi demanded. "The lying son of a bitch will say anything to save his worthless ass."

"Give him a chance."

"Look, you've got to understand," Jeffler pleaded. His eyes were beginning to well with tears. "I got sucked into all this. I know it's not much of an excuse, but my brother... I don't know, he just asked for this one favor, and there was a lot of money in it. And it seemed so easy, I, I just got carried away."

"People have already died because you got 'carried away,'" Grimaldi reminded him. "And the odds are a lot more are going to die before this is all done. So spare us the sob stories. You want to save yourself, start talking."

"I'm telling you, I don't know that much."

"Have you ever heard of a man called Frederick Sigfreid?" Bolan asked.

Jeffler shook his head. "No."

"How many different groups was your brother dealing stuff to?"

"Groups? I'm not sure—"

"Think about it, damn it!" Grimaldi jabbed Jeffler with his crutch again, this time much harder.

"All right. All right!"

"We know some stuff went to a bike gang," Bolan said. "The Renegades. They worked at Sanicorp with your brother. They also had a lab set up at Farthing Meadows Cemetery, in the tunnels that used to run between buildings when it was an asylum. I think that somebody who used to work at the asylum tipped them off on the tunnels, and I think that same somebody was taking a share of everything being smuggled out of Gerley Chemical. Does any of this mean anything to you?"

Jeffler took a deep breath, trying to bring himself under control. In the distance he and the others could see flashing lights out on the highway, along with the sirens of the approaching ambulance.

"Look," he said, his voice cracking as he eyed his questioners. "I know about the bikers, and I know that my brother mentioned something about Bolivia in terms of the biochemical stuff, but—"

"All right, now we're getting somewhere," Grimaldi murmured.

"What about the Bolivians?" Bolan asked. "Any names? Places?"

Jeffler shook his head. "No. Todd clammed up the one time he mentioned them, like he hadn't planned on even letting me know that much."

"Come on," Bolan pressed. "This has been going on for months. He was your brother. He had to have mentioned more."

"I'm trying to think," Jeffler insisted. "But like I said, he... Hey, wait! You know, I *do* remember something. It was a couple months...no, that wasn't about the Bolivians."

"What?" Grimaldi said.

"It was one of the drug shipments," Jeffler recalled. "I remember there were a lot of synthetic hallucinogens in one shipment, and I made some crack about him dealing with hippies in Haight-Ashbury or something. And he said no, he wasn't dealing with dropouts. He said it was for students at some college. No, not a college. An institute. The Better Way Institute, something like that."

"Beta," Bolan said. "Beta Institute."

"I don't know." Jeffler shrugged. "Maybe that was it."

The Executioner traded glances with Grimaldi. "Bingo."

18

Grimaldi set down the Bell chopper in the lower parking lot of the youth camp located next door to the Beta Institute. Bolan unsnapped his seat harness and started to get out.

"Okay," he told Grimaldi, "give me an hour. If you haven't heard from me, then—"

"Ix-nay," Grimaldi said as he turned off the copter's engine. "I'm coming with you."

"Jack, forget it. Your leg."

"What about it?"

"The doctor said to stay on crutches until—"

"The hell I will!" Grimaldi climbed out of his seat and opened his door. "Let's go."

Bolan couldn't help but grin at the pilot's stubborn resolve. "I should have known."

The men unholstered their handguns and attached silencers as they stole through the camp, sidestepping heaps of unraked leaves strewn across the grounds. Grimaldi hobbled slightly, favoring his wounded leg.

Closed for the winter, the camp was eerily silent. Moonlight shone on bunkhouses with boarded windows; idle swing sets and gym equipment cast long shadows on a grassy play area.

Separating the camp from the institute was a tall stone wall covered with a thick layer of ivy. When they reached the base of it, Bolan reached up through the leaves and tested the strength of a half-inch-thick runner. It held under his weight.

"This will work," Bolan said, slipping his gun back in its holster so he could climb with both hands. "You going to be able to manage?" he asked Grimaldi.

"Piece of cake."

As they neared the top of the wall, Bolan told his partner, "I'll bet their security force is armed with more than rubber bullets, so be careful."

"Always am," Grimaldi replied. "Ready when you are."

"Okay..."

In unison, the men pulled themselves up the last few feet and peered over the top of the wall. They were about fifty yards away from the nearest buildings. Directly below them on the other side of the wall was an unbroken row of untrimmed wild rosebushes, devoid of leaves or flowers but clearly festooned with thorns. It was obviously intended as a barrier against those who might be thinking of escaping from the institute, but it also posed an equal hazard to Bolan and Grimaldi in terms of getting down from the wall.

"Broad jump, anyone?" Grimaldi muttered, sizing up the situation.

"That's how I'm going," Bolan said. "You can forget it, though. And that's an order."

Even Grimaldi wasn't foolhardy enough to think he could make the jump without severely reinjuring his leg. He glanced down the length of the wall in both directions, trying to figure out an alternative plan.

"Okay, tell you what," he said finally. "You go ahead and hop down here. I'll backtrack down to the lake and circle around."

"Sounds good. Where do we meet?"

The Stony Man pilot pointed to a building near the lakefront. "How about that boat house?"

"Done."

As Grimaldi lowered himself back down the wall, Bolan precariously straddled the top, then crouched at the knees. Straightening his legs, he sprang forward, gaining enough momentum to clear the rosebushes. He landed hard, breaking his fall by tumbling with the expert grace of a seasoned paratrooper. In a matter of seconds, he was back on his feet, Beretta in hand.

And not a moment too soon, either.

Bolan had taken only a single step forward when he heard a rustling in the brush off to his left. Whirling, he leveled his gun at a security guard who stepped out from behind a tree. The guard had his finger on the trigger of a Belgian FN rifle, but he hesitated a moment, and that was all Bolan needed to neutralize him with a single shot from his Beretta.

The warrior rushed to the fallen guard and quickly checked the rifle. As he suspected, the 20-round magazine was filled, not with relatively benign rubber bullets, but with live 7.62 mm ammo.

If there had been any doubts before, they were eliminated now. He had engaged the enemy, and the enemy was playing for keeps.

THE WATER WAS numbingly cold, but Grimaldi wasn't about to rush. The lake was calm now, and any rapid slogging through the water would only give himself away.

The wall between the institute and the summer camp extended a dozen yards out into Lake Jeltz, and Grimaldi could smell the pungent buildup of algae on the mortared stone. The water deepened dramatically with every slow step he took, and by the time he reached the end of the wall, he was dog-paddling to stay afloat.

Once he'd circumvented the wall and was on institute property, Grimaldi stayed put in the water a moment, peering ashore. His view was partially obstructed by a pier that reached out into the water. He couldn't see the section of wall Bolan had scaled, so there was no way to tell if the Executioner was safely on the ground and advancing to their rendezvous. There were numerous halogen security lamps spaced about the grounds, bathing the terrain in a surreal yellow hue. Fifty yards inland, Grimaldi spotted a guard standing vigil near the boat house where he was supposed to catch up with Bolan.

A second sentry paced along the pier, his back to Grimaldi. The man had a rifle cradled in his arms, and in the deathly silence, the pilot could hear the guard humming to himself. The sound carried so clearly that Grimaldi was even more apprehensive about moving toward shore. But he couldn't stay where he was much longer. He was losing sensation in his fingertips and toes.

Mercifully a fisherman some two hundred yards east of the pier decided to call it a night and started up his small boat's motor, drawing the sentry's gaze and sending a high-pitched whine across the surface of the lake. Grimaldi took advantage of the diversion and stealthily stroked his way to the far end of the pier. Glancing up through the wooden planks, he could see the guard without himself being seen. From this new position he also had a clearer view ashore. Straining his eyes, he was finally able to make out Bolan's furtive movement through a stand of small pines between the wall and the boat house. By the same token, Grimaldi realized that if the sentry were to take a closer look, he might spot Bolan as well.

The fisherman's motorboat revved its way toward the pier, apparently intent on making a beeline to a launch located on the other side of the lake. The surface of the water rippled from the motor's wake, providing Grimaldi with cover as he inched his way to a wooden ladder extending into the water down from the pier. Once he had one hand on the ladder's rungs, Grimaldi drew his Colt .45. He held his breath, hoping the fisherman wouldn't spot him and relay an inadvertent warning to the sentry.

As the motorboat headed directly past the pier, Grimaldi made his move. He pulled himself from the water and cleared the final rung of the ladder. He had both feet on the pier before the sentry was able to hear him over the drone of the motorboat. He started to turn, but the Stony Man pilot was already on top of him. Clamping one hand over the sentry's mouth, Grimaldi knocked the guard out with a well-placed blow to the back of the head. He quickly lowered the man's limp form to the planks, then glanced toward shore.

Bolan had broken from cover as well, and Grimaldi saw him slip across a few yards of clearing to the boat house, then creep up behind the other guard and overpower him.

"Nice," Grimaldi whispered. He hurried ashore, reaching the boat house just as Bolan was interrogating the man he'd pinned to the ground. It was a teenage boy, and he looked terrified.

"We're here for the unofficial tour," Bolan told the youth. "And you're going to be our guide."

19

Rosey Tosca couldn't have felt worse if he'd died and gone to hell.

Within a few seconds of returning to consciousness, he realized he was in one of the observation rooms in the subterranean laboratory at the Beta Institute. And he wasn't alone. Standing in front of the door was Jax Allmus, arms crossed in front of his chest, a look of cold malice on his features. Dr. Dykes was in the room, too, huddled over a table set next to the far wall.

And there was a third man as well.

Jimmy Bariggia.

Not your typical don, not by a long shot. Still a year or two shy of his fortieth birthday, Bariggia stood six feet tall and weighed under two hundred pounds, most of it in top condition thanks to regular workouts at his nephew's athletic club. He wore a simple gray suit, blue shirt and no tie. He greeted Tosca with a smile.

"Rosey," he called out cheerfully. "How's my boy?"

Tosca didn't answer. None of this made any sense. In recent months he'd had dealings with all three of these men, but always under separate circumstances, with none of them supposedly aware of Tosca's links with the others. And yet here they were, obviously acquainted, apparently drawn into some kind of unholy alliance.

"Now, now, Rosey. What's the matter? Cat got your tongue?" Bariggia chuckled as he nonchalantly strolled over to the corner of the room where Tosca lay on the floor. The smile was still on the don's face when he suddenly lashed out with the tip of his shoe, stabbing his toe into Tosca's ribs. The hardman groaned as the pain cut through the steady ache he'd already been feeling. He felt nauseous and turned away from Bariggia. The don wouldn't have any part of it, though. He clamped his hand over Tosca's mouth and leaned forward, pinning Tosca's back to the floor. With his other hand, Bariggia whipped out a switchblade and sprang the gleaming edge into view.

"Puke on my hand and I'm going to be the one who has your tongue, not the fucking cat," he warned Tosca. "Understand?"

As Tosca fought back his nausea, there was a part of him that felt it would be in his best interests to not only go ahead and vomit, but also to resist Bariggia as violently as possible. With any luck he'd be killed instantly and spared the horrors that he was certain lay ahead. He was too weak to put up much of a fight, though, and when he tried to move his arms and legs he realized he was tightly bound at the wrists and ankles.

Bariggia gave his wrist a quick, almost imperceptible flick. Light from the overhead lamp reflected off the switchblade as it skimmed across Tosca's face, drawing blood from a thin slash on his cheekbone.

"You know, Rosey," Bariggia said as he stood and wiped the blade clean on a handkerchief, "the sad thing about all this is that it didn't even have to happen. I mean, all you would have had to do was play straight with me. But no, you figure that since I'm still cutting deals with the Medellín cartel, I wouldn't be interested in doing business with Mr. Allmus here.

"Or maybe that wasn't it at all, eh? Maybe you *knew* I'd be interested, but you didn't want to cut me in. Maybe you figured that if you helped the Bolivians set up shop in Detroit, they could push the Colombians out and then you'd be a real big shot, just like me. Hey, am I getting warm here, Rosey? Talk to me."

Tosca swallowed hard. His throat felt tight, his vocal cords strained. Still, he tried to force the words out. Tell him anything, he thought to himself. Tell him anything."

"I—I wanted to have things set up first," he said hoarsely. "It was going to be . . . like a gift."

Bariggia glanced at Allmus, a mirthful sparkle in his eye. "A gift? Is that right?"

Allmus shook his head. His expression remained humorless. "He never mentioned anything about a gift."

"Jimmy, listen," Tosca pleaded. "I know how uncertain things were with your Medellín connections. They could have fallen through completely at any time. They still might. You know that. I know that. Allmus knows that, too. I just wanted to be sure he was really ready to step in and handle the supply end on a large scale."

"Liar!" Allmus yelled across the room. "You told me that you had your own people. That you didn't need Bariggia. That you could give me a better price if I agreed to bring stuff in only through you, regardless of what happened with Medellín."

"No, I never said any of that!" Tosca insisted.

"You sure as hell did!"

Before the argument could escalate, Dykes turned away from the table and shouted, "Enough!"

When he had everyone's attention, he told them calmly, "There's no need for all this name-calling and accusing. I know how to make certain Mr. Tosca is telling us the truth."

Tosca glanced at Dykes and realized he was holding a hypodermic needle.

"This serum is a little different than the one that claimed my last patient," Dykes told the prisoner. "With any luck, you'll not only tell us everything you know, but you'll also manage to survive the side effects...."

FRANKIE CERDAE, Jax Allmus's Bolivian chauffeur and two of Jimmy Bariggia's bodyguards were milling about outside the observation room. Between the four of them, they'd racked up more than fifty murders in the service of their employers over the years, and behind the thin veneer of their supposed boredom lurked a homicidal vigilance. There was a mutual distrust between all parties, and should something go awry inside the adjacent room, all four men could be counted on to have their guns out and firing in a matter of seconds.

Something, in fact, did go awry, but not in the observation room.

The four gunmen shifted their attention to the far doorway as one of the institute's uniformed security guards strode into the antechamber.

"I need to speak to the doctor," the man said. "It's urgent."

"He's busy," Cerdae replied. Taking a closer look at the guard, he frowned. "Wait a second. I haven't seen you on patrol here before."

"I'm new." The uniform was a little tight on Bolan, but he still had full mobility and was able to draw his Beretta before any of the others could react.

"Everybody stay put," Bolan advised. Behind him, Grimaldi limped into the room, brandishing one of the Belgian FN rifles.

One of Bariggia's bodyguards was standing near a gurney. He leaned forward, shoving the cart with his thigh. As it rolled across the room toward Bolan, the guard leaped to one side, reaching inside his coat.

Bolan, not so easily distracted, fired and killed the man before he could draw his gun.

The war was on.

The other three bodyguards went for their weapons as they scrambled for cover. Bolan drilled Allmus's chauffeur, then dived to his right as Frankie Cerdae blasted away with his automatic, drilling huge holes in the tile walls behind the Executioner.

Grimaldi retreated to the doorway, partially shielding himself as he strafed the gathered enemy in the antechamber. He managed to drop Bariggia's second bodyguard and a stream of errant 7.62 mm rounds shattered the two-way mirror of the observation room, inadvertently wounding Dr. Dykes.

Inside the other room, Allmus pulled out a mini-Uzi and joined the fray, firing back out the shattered window. Grimaldi withdrew behind the doorway as 9 mm gunfire stitched the wall in front of him.

Bolan sighted Allmus and squeezed off a 3-round death blast, connecting twice with his target. One shot ravaged the Bolivian's shoulder, the other tore through his throat. Allmus dropped from view, but the Executioner felt certain he was dead.

Cerdae tried to take Bolan out at the same time he broke from cover and bolted for the back corridor. He missed the warrior but managed to reach the hallway. Before he could reach the steps, however, Grimaldi charged back into the chamber and brought him down with a volley from the Belgian FN.

The laboratory fell silent. Bolan and Grimaldi warily approached the observation room, sidestepping the fallen guards. Signaling back and forth, Bolan indicated he'd take the door. Grimaldi set down the rifle in favor of his Government Model .45 and inched toward the shattered window.

"Don't shoot," Jimmy Bariggia called out from inside the room. "We surrender."

Neither Bolan nor Grimaldi were about to take the man at his word, however. They closed in on the room, then the warrior charged in through the door as Grimaldi hurdled in through the window.

Allmus lay in a dead sprawl close to where Grimaldi had entered the room. Jimmy Bariggia stood in the far corner, hands in the air. He was more than willing to give up the fight for now, knowing full well that his lawyers would have a better chance of ensuring his freedom than any attempt to resist the gunmen before him.

Tosca was on the floor, barely conscious, the hypodermic needle still embedded in his right arm. Dykes was crouched over nearby, his lab coat and the side of his face red with blood from cuts caused by flying shards of broken mirror.

Bolan walked over to Dykes and jerked him to his feet, saying, "Dr. Sigfreid, I presume."

EPILOGUE

Allmus was dead, and Bariggia wasn't about to talk to the authorities. Dr. Dykes offered a partial confession, however, and with his veins flowing with truth serum, Rosey Tosca was more than willing to piece together those parts of the puzzle Bolan and the others had yet to piece together. By the time Bolan and Grimaldi had returned to Mosenan Isle to pass along the information to Hal Brognola, it had all fallen into place.

"After Sigfreid fled to Europe," Bolan related, "he changed his name and found work for a pharmaceutical firm in East Germany. Apparently he kept up his mind-control research on the side, and once he thought he was on the verge of a breakthrough, he slipped back into the States and started up the Beta Institute as a front for his experimenting.

"We know for a fact that Tosca and Ken Bridony procured teenage runaways as human guinea pigs for Sigfreid, and there might have been a few others."

"I see," Brognola said. "And it was Tosca who killed Bridony and Don White on Halloween night."

"Right. He killed Bridony because he knew the cops already suspected him in the kidnapping of the flower vendors, and he figured with enough planted evidence, it'd be easy enough to have Bridony take the rap for the Simmons murders, too."

"And those were committed by Tosca and Todd Jeffler."

"Right," Bolan agreed.

Brognola busied himself with another one of his omnipresent unlighted cigars, pacing before a window overlooking the Detroit River. It wasn't his nature to give in to euphoria, but there was no denying that overall this mission had succeeded far beyond its initial parameters. In addition to sealing the security leak at Gerley Chemical, the men of Stony Man Farm had also shut down the Renegades' drug ring, exposed illegal toxic-waste dumping by Sanicorp, blown the lid off the Beta Institute's clandestine mind-control experiments, and delivered a key blow to the Bolivians' attempt to supplant the Medellín cartel as czars of the international cocaine trade. And even if Jimmy Bariggia's battery of lawyers managed to wriggle him off the hook, the crime Family's activities in and around Motown had been unearthed to the extent that it would take them years to recover.

"All in all," he finally pronounced, "I'd have to say we put in a few days of good work."

"What next?" Bolan wanted to know.

"Well, Sheriff Hough's out of the hospital and he's gotten his hands on some extra tickets to the Lions game this weekend. They're playing the Redskins, so it should be a decent game. Able Team's already told me they'd like to hang around to see it. How about we all go?''

"Okay by me," Grimaldi said.

"I'll pass—so to speak," Bolan said, heading for the door.

"Where are you going?"

"I thought I'd drop by and see Helena. She wants to catch up on everything so she can start work on a couple stories for the next issue of the magazine."

"Oh, strictly business, right?" Brognola said.

Bolan grinned. "Right . . ."

ATTENTION ALL ACTION ADVENTURE FANS!

In 1994, the Gold Eagle team will unveil a new action-packed publishing program, giving readers even more of what they want! Starting in February, get in on even *more* SuperBolan, Stony Man and DEATHLANDS titles!

The Lineup:

- MACK BOLAN—THE EXECUTIONER will continue with one explosive book per month.

- In addition, Gold Eagle will bring you alternating months of longer-length SuperBolan and Stony Man titles—always a surefire hit!

- Rounding out every month's action is a *second* longer-length title—experience the top-notch excitement that such series as DEATHLANDS, EARTHBLOOD and JAKE STRAIT all deliver!

Post-holocaust, paramilitary, future fiction— Gold Eagle delivers it all! And now with two longer-length titles each and every month, there's even more action-packed adventure for readers to enjoy!

CATCH THE FIRE OF GOLD EAGLE ACTION IN 1994!

NEW

Take
4 explosive books
plus a
mystery bonus
FREE